There was once a  local to Vancouver, whos support of the arts, and the opening his radio show to a yearly poetry contest.

I gathered the courage to read my offering on the air, placing second, while the judge wondered aloud, if mine could be the work of a twelve year old boy. Mr. Murphy, however, was very supportive, even requesting that I send a copy for addition to his private collection.

It was inspiring, but true to my nature, and that of most children, I let the thought go, and my enthusiasm for word smithing fade away. Decades passed, until the necessity to write original scenes for an acting group, put me back in touch with this old friend I'd forgotten; the creation of the written word.

In a few years, serious study would result, in which I was fortunate to receive powerful guidance in English Literature. Starting with Prof. Charles Nelson, I benefitted from contact with a solid group of great, and inspirational Professors, at Langara College. If there is any power in my works, it is largely because of them.

In addition, I have since made the acquaintance of people learned in the craft, whose opinions I greatly respect. Couple these, with folk who simply have faith in my endeavors, and I consider myself a lucky man.

It is to all of these people, that I dedicate this book, and to you, my current reader.

Thank you all.

W.A. Salmon

Printed in Victoria, Canada

National Library of Canada Cataloguing in Publication

Salmon, W. A. (William Alan), 1960-
     Meanderings / W.A. Salmon.
Poems.
ISBN 1-55395-297-9
     I. Title.
PS8587.A3546M42 2002   C811'.6   C2002-905596-2
R9199.4.S35M42 2002

TRAFFORD

This book was published *on-demand* in cooperation with Trafford Publishing.
On-demand publishing is a unique process and service of making a book available for retail sale to the public taking advantage of on-demand manufacturing and Internet marketing.
On-demand publishing includes promotions, retail sales, manufacturing, order fulfilment, accounting and collecting royalties on behalf of the author.

Suite 6E, 2333 Government St., Victoria, B.C. V8T 4P4, CANADA
Phone   250-383-6864   Toll-free   1-888-232-4444 (Canada & US)
Fax   250-383-6804   E-mail   sales@trafford.com
Web site   www.trafford.com   TRAFFORD PUBLISHING IS A DIVISION OF TRAFFORD HOLDINGS LTD.
Trafford Catalogue #02-1011   www.trafford.com/robots/02-1011.html

10   9   8   7   6   5   4   3   2   1

LIST OF 62 POEMS

Glastonbury Tor
The Unlucky One
Sarah
The Fall of Kings
You Know It
What the Ocean Brings
Entity Identity
Women of Vendee - 1793
A Distant Cry
"D"
Northwesterners
Futility
Celtic Patterns
Watching Our Sunset
Gathering of Comrades
Silence
Gliding in Wilderness
Old Friends
Stroller Blossom
Warriors of the Fire Sword
Summer Girl
Keeper of the Unicorn
Between the After
Shutters
Daughter of Venus
Farewell
The Echo Strikes
Bridge to Tintagel
I Recall Scotland
Farewell - The Warrior
Lost Treasure
Scotti Fare
Simple Fox
Wings of Faith
It Takes Me

The Mask
Cold March
Michelle
Final Stand
Mead
Memories of a Robin
She
A Feather Floating
Desert Vipers
Candle Wax
The Star
The Long Mist Waltz
Tintagel
Yours
By George
 Somerset
Eclipse
Haunting
This I know
The Owl
Lighthouse Keeper
Where's Igor
Melting
The Kill
Scrape of the Timber
Soft Goes the Drummin
Mared's Hope

SHORT FICTION

Troll and Maiden
Spilt Milk
One Photo
Old Guard
Heartless
Where's the Fire
Dig
On a Pressing Problem

GLASTONBURY TOR

Tor - some kind of ancient man
sits here.
Where do I go, now that my soul
was born
somewhere back there?
Now there's a haze in your kindled slits,
and your stones are fused by dimming light.
Sit back, and watch the sea appear,
while sheep call out to coming night.
Oh yes - way back when I was young,
before the blind cold light.
To waking stars I simply whisper,
'Time to sing in flight!'

THE UNLUCKY ONE

He feels the slash of horses' wings
Honey sweet on wispy water
Rainbow thoughts are born on gold spill
Sighing life brings greetings
from a jaded mat.
Suddenly cast beneath the cloak
of the dire life taker
no hope - no mirth
it comes brooding - untouchable.

Upon the grounds, and round the manor
while the geese do fuss, and clamor
the victim's bane is heard to stammer,
"My God! It's my own poison!"

SARAH

Some years ago
where I had grown
life was full with
dear hearts I'd known.
Quite a lad I was
with my girl in hand
as down Glasgow roads
we'd stroll for hours.
In garden's bloom
or neath the moon
life was so fine with
Sarah.

She was tall
and she was wild
with hair that matched
the raven's wing.
And skin cream white
like a Celtic queen
a lively blossom
she had become.
To think we'd fought
through childhood cold
and I'd curse the name of
Sarah

In starlight's veil
our bodies would glisten
as we'd glide o'er each other
in passion's grasp.
She'd giggle and whisper
then kiss me so long
as the moon fled away
from the coming dawn.
Amid new earthen fragrance
and the waking bird's song
I'd breath the name of
Sarah.

Her Kinsmen blamed me
for her sudden condition
and I realized the manly life
that I was missing.
So I faded into
the scarlet ranks
they gave me shelter
and I offered them thanks.
As Wellington's top man
I could come back again
and care for my dear one
Sarah.

In Spain with the Seventh
I battled hard thrice
and glory came
with a grisly price.
But the ladies were plenty
and the women were willing
and battlefield wives
came with the shilling.
Yes we looked so fine
with our women and wine
that I scarcely remembered
my home.

'Live life to the fullest
for you may not see tomorrow'
I remembered those words
as cruelly my blood flowed.
The sun baked that valley
near Salamanca town.
The French had held strong
in shooting us down
while no others came
to help us.

Where men were dead
and I thought I was dying
as musketry stopped
when the sun was high.
So they came closer
to loot their kills
twas then that I saw
the bold Cuirassier.
He rode near on a
glistening black horse
dismounted then drew sword
smiling at me.

Too weak to fight on
I lay still and stared
as he hissed, "Adieu Anglais"
with huge square teeth bared.
And I realized the manly life
that I was missing
while his sword seemed to rise
so far above.
Then my final thoughts
brought tears to my eyes
and I breathed a single word
"Sarah."

THE FALL OF KINGS

Why are Kings reduced thus?
To stand amongst the rabble,
waiting for scraps left by
the scrabbling mass.

Their quivering brows tell of troubled times
and yet, there's power in golden eyes,
while little can dim their sturdy crowns
of ivory down.

Still, they wait
I hate to think why;
much closer to me, than to the sky;
much closer to me than I deserve,
ignoring the scavenger's cry.
Amid the stench, where nothing belongs;
again, I hate to think why.

YOU KNOW IT

To face the world
on its' own terms
and clear life's hurdles
free of harm
I'd meet each challenge
so strong of heart
if my van
would only start!

WHAT THE OCEAN BRINGS

Before my eyes in lapping jade
lolling specters glide, and fade
o'er hungry stars who slow graze
on boulders dark, and eerie.

And out beyond the inbound waves
life goes on in time's deep haze,
where storms are born to want, and rage,
till mellow age does spend them.

There's something about a ship at sea
brought to cruel fangs by squalls, and shrieks
with timber's roar, and sailor's screams
hushed; by kisses briny.

Then all join in the spectral dance
where some men's eyes do stare askance,
and bits of wood do swirl, and prance
like stars, before my eyes.

ENTITY IDENTITY

I am the enemy
of myself
in hatreds' thriving pastures
of ebony stalks
shining in shadow
a crown of clouds broiling
on a stolid brow
and eyes of diamond set
warming the land
in an inferno of ice
where the weak find comfort
in redirecting sorrow.

WOMEN OF VENDEE 1793

Women on the River Loire
I hear your cries for mercy now,
ignored by those who brought your pain
by virtue of good Robespiere.
Don't bother to shout
your pleas are drowned,
while fireworks wash
vile deeds from years.
No eyes will watch,
as they rip you naked
you survivors of the struggle doomed
spared the bayoneted womb.
On they lead you to the river
who was raped, and who was left?
Into the boats, your bodies herded;
perhaps the slaughtered were truly blessed.
Women in the River Loire
hold not the water from your lungs,
for if you do, they'll run pikes through
your bared, bruised, battered breasts.
So glide downstream like good French girls;
rise not again, to see the Sun,
so France can cheer with smiles, and tears
for a Great revolution won.

A DISTANT CRY

A soul in bondage
cold grey skin
its' voice so distant - like a faded memory
calling faintly in the night.

Like an Orca
plying a lonely path
having lost it's pod - forever calling; never answered
ne'er a ripple in chilling flight.

The pitiful grieving
of a wild thing
bowed over it's fallen mate - refusing to leave
though horrid death hovers.

And I sit
safely isolated
embraced by emptiness - comforted by silence
defeated by one distant cry.

"D"

She of the hunt
went roaming one night
a fine feast, and gems
brought her delight
and just when a peaceful
green glade was in sight
the wolves came on snarling
to put her to flight.

And by the thirteenth
beat of the sun
they all pounced, and smashed her
so suddenly gone
to leave us considering
why tears freely fell
and wanting to see the wolves
all bound for hell.

Perhaps twas her grace
bringing everyone pride
offering a rainbow
for the wretched to ride
or her golden smile kindling
dim hearts cast aside
or the day she bedazzled
as a radiant bride.

But, the bells tolled so slowly
wailing hemmed her last path
such bright colors sailing
on a fading cannon blast
like a sun's ray to glide
north, where rose petals fall
and shine forth in peace
from a lone, silent isle.

NORWESTERNERS

Born in the shadow of mountains
pioneer's deeds still ripple the waters
pioneer spirit does ripple the blood.

Our winds tell us secrets no others can hear
pines sing their songs for the mountain born
pines cool the reaching minds of their kin.

Our hearts keep time with the dance of the moon
the eagles' flight carries our thoughts
the eagles' wings caress our souls.

We are a different folk for all this
born of these western lands
born of the alpine glow.

Take pride in the difference of our kin
know the strength of our land, and soul
know why the eagles fly.

FUTILITY

Every man is different
everyone's the same
Every woman's different
everyone's the same
In clouds, and sea, and turf clods
downward slashing canes
Forever seeking pockets
for squared, and rounded frames
Flowers, flowers, blades of grass
which ones shall we blame?

CELTIC PATTERNS

Might, and Mercy
Honor honest
hot fury from
the kindest soul
Stubborn wags
an agreeable tongue
loud with humor
sparse words in rage.
No simple pattern
pleases the eye
simple tales
find deaf ears
simplicity discarded
trampled into mud
a greater dimension
forever sought
On, and on
intricate lines
guiding us forth
to the Celtic Heart.

WATCHING OUR SUNSET

If you should pass across the sea
I know the pit shall come to me.
And in my breast a lava stone
where once there reigned a blazing rose.
Then ice shall form within my mind
while in this world I shall walk blind.
The raven's call shall strike me deaf
I'll seek your form and find no rest.
No comfort found in pungent Spring
here while your ghost is lingering,
like failing rays of our dying day
upon my lonely pond.

GATHERING OF COMRADES

Now come, and have a drink lad,
though the shelling's made you mute.
There'll be no never mindin'
if there's mud upon upon your boot.
For we all stood together,
where the shells, and bullets flew.

The shining's for the peacetime;
we march now from the fens.
Where some have found their last steps,
and some won't march again,
and some will hear so far away
of the valor on which they depend.

And the cost to all, across the miles;
now the mess aint far away.
We'll gather there, and drink a toast
on our dear Remembrance Day.

SILENCE

I need Silence!
Silence!
Silence to think
Silence to aim
Silence to dream
and dream of Silence!

I'll shut up now
Now!
Before you start
Complaining, and
Glaring, and Wishing
and Praying for Silence!

GLIDING IN WILDERNESS

Gliding in wilderness
Aqua Marine
frozen in time moving
forever slowly
Killer Whales leap showing
how much they've grown
trusting in us to still
triggers, and shutters
superior beings standing
alone
When we make mistakes
they simply must pay
when we nod our heads
they may swim away
And our buttons won't squat
freezing our worlds in time
swiftly expanding
a glorious plant standing
against the night sky

Gliding through wilderness
as black as coal
showing the galaxy
how much we've grown
trusting the void
to remember us well
stuck in ruined amber
a portrait of hell

OLD FRIENDS

We'll meet at a place like the Mitre,
when we're mellow friends, grey, and old.
And I shall smile over my cane;
you'll be resplendent in our autumn gold.

And we'll know that frost shall cover all
born in this year's changing winds,
while wilting roses shall not see
the spring we know will come again.

But, we've known spring once, and that's enough,
for every life has dew, and dust,
yet the sun shall bring a shimmering day
o'er springtime's green, or winter's grey.

We'll grin, and laugh, and shine so warm,
through days that may not dawn again.
We'll talk of all that's gone before;
adventures bringing joy, and pain.

I hope our backs won't bow too much,
but we wouldn't notice - defiance in our eyes.
Talking of so much to come;
the fare of life to fire our years.

Yes, I think we'll meet at the Mitre,
and I shall smile over my cane.
Let's have a pint to scare the young,
and have fun being bold again!

STROLLER BLOSSOM

She was a beautiful girl
on a subway train.
She couldn't have been
much more than one year old.
At times she'd look thoughtful
as her father reached down,
to keep her finger from her nose,
while she looked up from the seat of earth.
And we stared down from lofty thought
floating beneath a universal cap,
offering handles for deities to grab,
all brooding in our superior reason.

She laughed, and smiled through radiant blue,
as she made a game of grabbing father's
hovering fingers, and many around smiled
in spite of themselves, in rigid, urban, formality.
But the eyes of the cheated rang hollow upon her;
drooping, as they cast a gaze down,
while innocence ripped into beating marble,
and laughter probed ancient wounds.
On a subway car, needing room
they found none, trying not to contact flesh,
but chose to stare across the heavens,
forced to think of children lost
by their choice
or another's.

WARRIORS OF THE FIRE SWORD

Imagine
A broad, and blazing shadow
like a blast - a vicious sunrise
a wound forever festering
never closed - searing the soul.

Imagine
Mighty nations welcoming dusk
which in turn never leaves,
but banishes the dawn
sending her weeping - in poverty with truth.

Imagine
A land of darkness, cold, and frost
numbing the mind - and soul
complacent ones ignore grit, and shadow
forgetting the warming glow.

See the Warrior
With flaming sword slashing mightily
striking down the dusk, and chill,
liberating joy, and hope
raising them up for all to feel.

See the darkness
Drawing the bow - it's thrum
amid our laughter, and cheer
sending its' swifting bolt of coal
to smite the Warrior - strike us numb.

See our grieving
The fall of that smoldering sword
ignited again by the grasp of the brother,
raising it up to remember the Warrior
and strive forth for his dream.

See the swift arm
Of shadow again - striking quickly
our next great hope in his puddle growing
round his head - "Don't touch me; don't touch me."
And the darkness returned to chill the bone.

Hear chains rattling
Holding sweet dawn in bondage
with truth, and hope fastened, to a dungeon wall
awaiting a champion to finally free them;
do they wait in vain? Who'll hear the call - and remember?

SUMMER GIRL

Her hair falls golden
upon breast, and brow
the summer sun kisses
soft cheeks in bloom

As a fawn
in meadow's glow
grace sired her there
in full lithe form

Away she glides
on morning mist
her beauty puts
amber rays to shame

Away she fades
to memory
never to
caress again

Her, and I
if only
in
my mind

KEEPER OF THE UNICORN

I once espied a Unicorn
a skirting round a field.
She whispered to my soul, and mind,
and she asked me to yield
Said she, "You are a warrior
so great, and strong, and bold;
please stay with me
that none may come,
and take my horn of gold!"
And so I did, and so she pranced
especially for me
but the flowers were so beautiful
I just had to stop to see
Her eyes shimmered upon me
as she offered me sweet song
but the buzz of bees was so strong
I just had to sing along
Her hooves they slowed so slightly
but I didn't realize
those bright clouds fairly shielded
that fire fading in her eyes
Her withers heaved, and trembled
as she staggered through those days
while the trees stood as majestic
as those mountains far away
She knelt upon the dusky grass
her head bowed by my side
and with a rolling rush of tears
the Unicorn just died.

I've roamed long since in hidden shame,
and wear a fair, fierce eye,
and I'll keep safe forevermore;
this horn of gold
hung by
my side.

BETWEEN THE AFTER

"What are you doing
with all those dog tags,
down here by the river -
watching?"

"I'm cleaning the gore
from these bright beaded chains,
so dear women won't see
their darling ones."

"You've been long in battle,
and seen all the glory;
now it's your own fingers
are putting it on."

"Is that why I couldn't
get them all clean?
God help me remember
I'm somebody's son!"

"Too late for the lonely
who've lost all our friends
down here by the river -
burying."

SHUTTERS

People walking down the street,
staring through windows;
some from castles
some from holes.

Plastic People
cannot see you
lest prestige come,
and ransom your soul.

There she offers a brilliant smile
an ornate key;
no window frame
to lean across.

The sneers forgotten
laughter takes wing;
the dirt is much cleaner
where I repose.

DAUGHTER OF VENUS

She stands, a statue
marble finish, eggshell skin
full of melted butter
writhing inconsolable
transfixed by a tear.

How do I touch her?
How do I help her?
How do I keep
from breaking her heart?

FAREWELL

Our homestead goes down,
and time goes on.
No scream did it sound;
now fallen, and gone.

All the Johnny-come-lately's
they don't give a damn,
as our years, and memories
get ground into sand.
A handful of foreigners
scream the command,
and...

Smiling old faces
are eaten by rust;
a childhood of Christmases
belched out in dust.
We've all become specters;
surrendered to crust,
and...

A homestead goes down;
more pioneers move on.
The new folk just smile;
the history gone.
I must turn away;
elsewhere I'm drawn.
Farewell to them all;
I'm gone - and on,
and on...

THE ECHO STRIKES

Carnations spread
upon springtime grey.
Hard thought lets them
drift away,
past mirrored vision
sighting - a galaxy breadth;
as far, as a scream can carry.
Within, and without,
on a Belfast street
amid the shouts.

And people running,
running,
heartbeats fill the air,
and last breaths chime the toll.
As the rage comes back;
a blinding echo, slicing sanity,
and the mirror drinks
sparing nothing.

BRIDGE TO TINTAGEL

Let us stand at Tintagel,
and watch brave Arthur's steed vault by.
And harken to great Merlin's words
below the gull's, and eagle's cry.
Away, away now we must go
beyond bold yesterday's coming deeds.
To stand upon these timeless shores.
To kiss the folk who never bleed.
And rise to slumber, honor bound,
until the trumpets sound again
at Prydain's waking need.

I RECALL SCOTLAND

I recall Scotland
on the windward, and lee
and wandered her 'spanse
over ben, dale, and stream
where the sun strikes blood red
over Killikrankie

Oh I recall Scotland
what a dear one to me.

Then to the bruised heights
of watchful MacDui
where silence comes greeting
and makes you believe
and old Aviemore
nestles green as can be

Oh I recall Scotland
what a dear one to me.

The Rock sits so stolid
over Edinburgh's streets
it's walls look so dark
where the powers still be
and the old witches' wail
brings the kilted armies

Oh I recall Scotland
such a fierce one to me

There's sweet Inverness
rolling out to the sea
where the wind sings through heather
and through thistle does scream
where the swift tartan pride
fell to foul musketry

At Culloden Moor
sullen o'er weeping sea.

Twas off to the Highlands
through the mild vale of Ness
where the tall sighing pines
offered deep easy rest
and tears somehow found me
where the lush green hills crest

Oh I recall Scotland
the land of the blessed.

And o'er peaceful waters
to the bright gem of Skye
a shimmering expanse
o'er which men raged, and died
and the elven folk watch
through a lone eagle's eyes

Oh I recall Scotland
Heaven's own bride.

Through Loch Lomand's silence
and Glasgow's twin pride
to Ayr's placid shores
and Stranraer's waiting pier
like so many before
borne across shielding sea
watching her go
to intense memory
Oh I'll ne'er again touch her
lest in visions, and dreams
oh I recall Scotland
such sweet majesty

Oh I recall Scotland
what a dear one to me!

FAREWELL - THE WARRIOR

When Donal died
the skies wept fully
three days long, with thunder mighty
as the man had been in life
A strength allowing silent pride.

I watched him there
upon mounting pyre
that bold heart stilled, gentle memories frozen
melting to droplets, clinging to clouds
Awaiting the fierce Valkyries' ride.

His faded laughter
soared through my mind
his noble soul deserving the journey
with no tears shed, I wished him well
And watched him glide.

LOST TREASURE

Cause to bend;
cause to break;
you'll find no salvation
in the eyes of a snake.
And nothing devours
like a gilded lie.
And whyfore is lost
where the maidens cry.

SCOTTI FARE

Down near the place where I live
there's a proud Scots piper standing;
living in two dimensions over
a steady neon beacon reading
'Open', and people wander past
before his dark restaurant doors.

Inside, they boast fine Scotti fare
in food, and island liqueurs, where a
clinging Celtic atmosphere hovers
above marbled Mediterranean mirrors,
while the waitresses speak Greek
'neath numerous coats of arms, and tartans.

It's a funny odd place to sit
for those who remember the Tuatha De Danann,
exchanging secret glances with old names, and colors
staring proudly down,
while an Asian cook struggles hard
over a grill, and fine Scotti fare.

SIMPLE FOX

Simple fox, why do you snarl?
With mounted neck you'll see no moon.
You couldn't win against them all.
I wonder, what was your last wound?

Oh to the moors just once again!
What secrets there you must have kept;
promises to pixies made
with eyes stuck open - do you sleep
to dream of freedom once ignored,
now on the "Three Crowns" smokey stones,
where I enjoy my Devon brew.
Oddly now I think of you.
I know in life you'd smile back
down 'pon a kindred flea.

WINGS OF FAITH

Take the flight of the eagle.
Defeat those bruised, and covetous clouds.
Stand on both sides of a razor.
Bare your spirit to the blade.
Let it pass through.
You'll not be cut.
No sting, but a twining
through faith.

Let diamond feathers
strive to slice you.
Let those winds shriek
as you plummet.
Know your wings will bear you,
though they feel broken - shattered.
The skies will speak, and bring you forth
upon your wings of faith.

IT TAKES ME

What is it?
This swift, and flitting cart
illusive at times,
but forever whisking me
suddenly
to my secret lands;
fathomless realms all nestled,
stalking between twilights,
and beyond.
Twisting, turning
teasing visions come to hunt,
or play
with phantom folk of cloud,
or shadow so real;
vibrant, then gone,
until I return.

THE MASK

The mask stares steadily
sternly
crevices adding weight
years give substance
eyes span space
stopping, striking, reflecting my soul
falling like starlight
casts aside the black hole
a void so devoid
it fills all.
But through it
is seen a familiar face
the mask reveals itself
after all as my friend.

COLD MARCH FOR A DYING MAN

Time, cruel time
what do you bring?

My heart beats,
while the clock chimes ring.

That ticking march
does drag me closer;

to forgotten ghosts
who dance, and sing.

To destiny, and
the grave embracing.

A precious pause
no purchase gaining.

Soon to feel
burdensome earth;

Heaped on by
spading chimes.

While me breath,
and blood are waning.

A chilling stranger
waits nearby grinning.

God, what has passed
into hungry mire;

Neath the belly
of serpentine time?

MICHELLE

The way she runs
in morning sun
a woman to bring
the woods to song

Her smile kindles
my ashen heart
a tallow candle's
steady glow

Her voice comes lightly
on the breeze
like harp strings strumming
sweet as mead

Her amber hair
does flow and shine
an aqua veil falling
misting below

And more than all
her chestnut eyes
do drink my soul
and hold me there in joy

FINAL STAND

In Burns Bog clings
a stand of pines.
Their mild scent fails
where methane forms.
Their needles rot
where trash piles high,
and the stench of man
overcomes all.

What have they seen
these living cells,
when natures' kingdom
stood so strong;
when myriad animals
wandered proudly,
and great dark warriors
spoke their words.

Then grinning sea gulls
humbly encroached
gaining their foothold
upon neutral sand;
raising modest cabins
as reverently as young,
while taking what they needed
and dreaming of their empire.

A tractor dances
upon glistening slime;
waltzing decay out
toward besieged life,
where centuries may die
by the setting sun.
In Burns Bog clings
a stand of pines.

MEAD

May the winds be fair
as your finest ale,
and the sun burn brightly,
as a fine swig of scotch.
May your eyes always sparkle
like a thick, dark stout,
and may you never run out
of sweet Mead!

For, many a warrior
this elixir has pleased,
from the honey of heather
in green highland hills.
If you reached up, and squeezed
the milk from heaven's breast,
the catch in your flask
would be Mead.

So, count your life
as truly blessed,
if Mead be sweet
as your woman's kiss,
and old you grow
in rosy bliss,
and die with fine Mead
passing your lips.

And when you reach
the other side,
raise your sword,
and hollow horn high,
then bring your woman
to the warrior's fire,
where we'll never run out
of sweet Mead.

MEMORIES OF A ROBIN
Or, Roadside Sacrifice

I saw a robin on the road
I had to swerve to miss it - there
crouching in the rain

I did not stop to see it
for its' pain may have - been
too great in me

I thought I saw its' agony
I thought I saw it chirping - screaming
pleading for kind mercy

I remember how it stared at me
I remember how it - trusted
in my kind heart

And I drove by deserting it
choosing to sacrifice it to art - immortal
in learned mankind

I did not pass that way again
for fear it might be flying well - to strike
me down in weak faith

It's a comfort to have kept driving
so I couldn't think too much about - the Robin
fading sorely in my mind

SHE

Having fun
with form
Yes -it is -yes
There
Rolling
Twirling
An Acrobat Queen
Rides on Hard Music
Round her stage before men
Cheering as her clothes are gone
And her artful moves hold some in awe
Respecting the poetry of a woman's form
Impossibly   Beautiful
Blessed   Sight
A Celebration
Of tawny flesh
Gracefully Carried
With glorious resistance
To gravity's burden
An elastic response as
She struts before us
Her bedroom glances
Surveying the crowd
Wondering if we
Could be the one
Who takes her
Home tonight!
But we'll
Stay put
Grinning
With
Fright!

A FEATHER FLOATING

The setting moon
gives way to dawn
and death defeated
calls the sun.
The twining burst,
and wings unfurled;
gales rush
to a forgotten world.

Swirls back to greet
each new one born,
alone - not lonely;
not to mourn.
But, breath, and fly
in peace again
upon a soothing
silent wind.

And ponder long
in rain's caress
how very difficult it is
to be a feather floating.

DESERT VIPERS

Hush now young one
don't you cry
at the sound of bullets
ripping by.

Swiftly now
they will get you
too soon to slumber
you'll go too.

Tomorrow's fighters
gone to ground
a generation
all cut down.

No hands to grasp
sweet freedoms' tools
and stand against
the righteous rule.

Of yesterday's victims
standing proud
denying others
hallowed ground.

With no one else
allowed to fight
they butcher you
by Divine Right.

CANDLE WAX

I am who I am not
Certain Striking
Ruby Crystalline
and clouded cream
in coffee secrets
beholding tea leaf promises
upon a cherry's gleam

For all that I behold
and all that I foretold
beyond the telling
at the ivory gate
where tiger's eyes do watch
through jade intentions fallen
and silent shrieks all singing
in speckled haze

A thousand soldiers
rattle tin
but none reveal
the one within
I close my eyes
within the din
a scattered oasis
yet - not crazed

Still
I am
Not
M
E
E
e
!

THE STAR

D. H. was a pretty one
I crossed tracks with in school
I was considered on the fringe
while she was oh so cool.

We hung around in Senior Shops
at Free Blocks in those days
to talk of all that we'd become
in worlds so far away.

And movie stars, we both would be,
though we would take paths separately,
and "see ya' in the movies"
was the way we parted there.

She went on to another school,
and never did we meet again.
Her memory still made me smile,
while I like to think I eased some pain.

The years went by still slowly,
while my acting slid to other things.
She was a happy memory,
then I saw a magazine.

She had grown to Angelic beauty;
her womanhood achieved,
still, I scarcely recognized
the girl I'd often seen.

Her new last name, and newfound fame
did bring her to the screen,
and everybody talked about
the girl I'd often seen.

But, then time passed too quickly,
and too soon I'd heard she died.
The bastard who had claimed her
blew her face off from the side.

I'd never planned to hunt a man;
hope I never will again,
but I sought a ticket to L.A.;
I didn't care what happened then.

Word quickly came, he'd killed himself,
and so I heaved a sigh,
although I'd lost a secret friend,
and had to wonder why.

Then 'What If's' came to haunt me.
Could I have won her heart?
Would she be alive today,
if I'd played a bigger part?

But, then her path may well have changed;
her quest for fame have failed;
so, I'm left to muse, and ask in vain;
Who can grasp a comet's tail?

THE LONG MIST WALTZ

Arthur reigns 'pon distant hill'
where bright knights charge, while ladies thrill,
and Avalon
stands oh, so still
awaiting her timeless Lord.

From Camlann's waste
just one would ride;
that greatest sword, cast to the tide.
His testament became my pride
to carry from shore to shore.

"You are a traveling Bard", he said.
His cloak was green
his eyes were red;
a rusted crown sat on his head,
and his shoes, a withered shroud.

Many a Lord are just like him,
who've lost the way in troubled realms,
and none to rule
in battle's din
among toppled, bloody helms.

King of Sunshine
King of pain
will you never wake again
near Avalon's sweet shores?

TINTAGEL

Where are your maidens
your young men in armor?
Whisper the waves on a comforting sea.

The winds are fast,
and swift clouds scream past,
but Tintagel's secrets tickle my ear.

Silence scolds
in the great rock folds
old powers command this violent breeze.

I hope for all
that our Arthur is well;
the babe of all, on Merlin's sleeve.

This, a cruel plan
for poor, fine Ygraine
giving the land it's sweetest seed.

Now the stars shine bright
on that blessed stone
in eternal sight, embracing me.

YOURS

Journey's beginning
Journey's end
To see the sky
and never bend
but take the path
without a step
a soul full spreading
through wings of light
then close our eyes
and feel our flight

BY GEORGE

A minstrel came a strolling
on gossamer fields with frozen streams
his fingers flew so lightly
like hawk's wings wet in mists of grey.

And the mists, they fled
so far to run as he reached up
to grasp the sun and light
those fields all round in verdant green.

Then bees, they came to light and greet
bright flower's bloom and music sweet
where streams did run
and whisper all their dreams.

Where blackbirds feast upon strawberry sheen
he paused to sup among them there
mid echoes of full twenty years
life's magic reflecting all that's learned.

But then he caught a withering wind
as cold as clay to take his song
but still, he played against the chill
to help our heartstrings ring.

Yet the sun it fled
and mists returned
ice traced brutish paths
while chill gusts burned.

But the minstrel smiled against his pain
dropped to one knee where his sitar lay
pointing to his distant orb which ne'er recedes
then he bowed, and softly

faded through felled leaves

SOMERSET

Thoughts of naught in diamond feathers
rise within a sailing eye of
green, and grey that trace the path
of Merlin's wink, and Arthur's stride.

The raven shall land where it may
here when these mists meander low,
through sleepy hills, and stones in rows
where once sparks flew from charging hooves.

And a staff once tapped, which won a crown,
then pulled the sun from neath mired reeds
to shine out from dear Camelot,
till shadows came, but still I see.

For I have walked the holy vale
and the green has sung to me.

ECLIPSE

An Angel stands
on parapet high, with naught
between herself, and sky

The Cloak of Doom
surrounds the sun
behind her, where gales scream

The Titan Sisters bow
and go to ground
with thunderous sigh

And Hell comes broiling
like ripples belching
quenching shrieks

Then Silence reigns
where bright winds mourn
Hope it fades, where Faith is born

Defiance mounts
a lightning steed, to grasp
the Torch of Liberty

And rise from Phoenix Ashes low
to ride the Breath of Glory
evermore

HAUNTING

I stand, a stranger
on my own
with ne'er a place
that feels like home
save one
when I stand before your eyes.

And when away
your face, it shines
in every corner
of my mind
and to my heart
an Angel's sing comes calling.

And in a blaze
of staggering blue
I shuffle on
in want of you
a melting heart
a million candles burning.

Yet heaven can
shift into hell
if from me your heart is held
but if we join
just in my dreams
I can stand the pain

So come, sweet phantom
for my mind needs haunting.

THIS I KNOW

I've dreamed your kiss a thousand times
searing nectar
takes my mind.

My soul is held, in glacial fire
the breadth of the sky
filling my being
till I could just fall in.

It is the sweetest twining
the softest lips in rising
It is the sweetest blessing
the beating of your heart 'gainst mine.

And time, it is defeated
it's ravages are cheated
within the power of our embrace.

We are forever; we are one
even though we've just begun
the whisperings of the jealous wind
they do concede, that we will win.

To joy, and glory
on the wing
in Sun's glow where
our souls shall sing.

A harmony
for the ages.

This I know.

THE OWL

Upon my perch
I see it all
the searching souls
and ones in thrall
with romance born
and ones forlorn
on the floor
where dreams are woven.

And if those dreams
are based on lust
and everything
just falls to dust
they have tonight
to smile, and trust
and find their own
sweet heaven.

A dancer shuffles
spilling beer
a beauty leaves
to hide her tears
my comfort held
I'll not come near
for I see all
around them.

Perhaps, sometime
I will watch you
in dreams newfound
and ones run through
with swivelling head
and talons true
in silence
where I found you.

Now who's
the proper scoundrel?

LIGHTHOUSE KEEPER

'Mid torrents
ripping in the night
the watcher stood
below his light
with hopeful gaze
throughout black haze
to where her voice
came calling.

The lantern
swung full to, and fro
in hopes to light
the surf below
across the shore
in bone deep cold
in quest of one
enthralling.

But she was
gone - the lady crowned
that tide did ebb
to leave him drowned
within that hollow
tolling sound
the curse
of a lone heart beating.

WHERE'S IGOR

They tie the spaniel down
and then spray shampoo in it's eyes
she shakes her head so violently
and yelps her piteous cry.

Then they come up, the clipboards
for there's not much they can say
just scrawl the 'no tears' product
is at least a year away.

A memo's sent off straight away
for perusal by the board
and mongrels with ruined vision
move off to the cancer ward.

And there they find new horror
all hope for them bereft
among mice, and other canines
full of tumors - close to death.

Throughout the place in cages full
so many realize
the nightmare that's upon them
you can see it in their eyes.

The newly caught, they vent their rage
in pounding at the bars
the broken tremble in their fate
minds raked, and bodies marred.

The tubes, they seem just like a chain
where pupils are quite spent.
"Dear, dear. The transplant didn't take;
the monkey is quite dead."

Clipboards come up, clipboards go down
white jackets just walk by
the chains are loosed, the body freed
that's one more they'll have to buy.

Then one more kick - an autopsy
to make sure it's all done right
then to the crematorium
the most merciful place in sight.

A trusting set of eyes arrives
so it begins again
where white coats bask in their great service
for the benefit of man.

MELTING

Beneath blue skies
two orbs, they rise
to probe where my heart bleeds.

I bow to taste
sweet mead below
my passion won't recede.

Ethereal wings
cross honey strands
like wind songs in the reeds.

I wait to say
that she is all
my spirits' greatest need.

And then she smiles
and all of me
goes melting.

THE KILL

The boulder's black
on which I sit
my blood is frozen still.

My bones all cracked
with creeping ice
and winds trace through them shrill.

For, now you've flown
away from me
your dagger drawn to kill.

The falcon o'er
the sparrow stripped
no more to glide, and trill.

My brain devoured
my guts displayed
all dreams flow cross the sill.

It rips, your beak
death flees my reek
the echo etched by will.

And if I could
just die, I would
but my veins just ebb, and fill.

SCRAPE OF THE TIMBER 'PON STONE

The wheel of the sun
came turning again
where shadow of moon
seeks to command
all fated to serve
sweet salvation's plan
in the scrape
of the timber 'pon stone.

I sit away
where few can see
besieged by powerful
memories
they hang him high
on Calvary
and so
he takes me home.

I shut my ears
to murderous screams
I scarcely note
the blood in streams
huge nails strike
so deep within
and shove aside
the bone.

Yet, it's scarce
a sound he makes
as the cross goes up
and muscles strain
when the base slams down
he'll not complain
in the fate
he's always known.

So near then
I can hear those words
which haunt my mind
and give me hope
"Remember me
in your kingdom Lord!"
"Truly
you'll be with me there."

And while they gamble
for his things
his breath grows short
and limbs sag numb
then see clouds gathering
broiling dark
and then he whispers
"It is done."

Still, they see fit
to break his legs
and pierce his heart
his torment done
and then clouds break
o'er shadowed lands
and lightning strikes
his killers dumb.

A bright bolt rips
the great curtain in twain
in the temple shaken
through it's throne
and torrents drive
the moaning mass
to wash away sin
but not that stone.

And there a lonely soldier stood
beneath the cross, with robe, and crown
to whisper words they would not say
"This truly was the Son of God!"
Then the few who were allowed
to take their Lord to Joseph's tomb
anoint him there in silence left
and so it begins!

Three days to walk
the terrors of hell
and none to touch
his radiant robes
but fly, and shriek
far from his sight
or sag, and weep
where his sandals fall.

Even the mightiest
watch him pass
none can begrudge
his victory won
so many who'd gone
before him freed
all march in praise
of the Holy One.

And so the slab
before him rolls
to let him stride
where soldiers sleep
with Angels whispering
in their ears
to keep them in
their sweetest dreams.

And then, to join
the happy few
and bring them hope
their strength renewed
no danger then
too great will be
when they remember
Calvary.

And how he walked
among them there
with death surpassed
and life reborn
there smiling down
where Angels swirl
to trumpet blasts
in shining clouds.

Thank God
for all sweet blessings gained
by the scrape
of the timber 'pon stone.

SOFT GOES THE DRUMMIN'

Soft goes the drummin' on the moor.

Cast back my mind
to another time,
when I was a young lout,
and a liar.

Soft goes the drummin' on the moor.

My theft fell short.
I watched him grin,
as he took his sword tip from my chin,
and bade me shelter in his tower.

Soft goes the drummin' on the moor.

Fast friends were we.
I'd stay at hand;
my loyalty at his command.
A sword he gave to guard his keep.

Soft goes the drummin' on the moor.

Another Warlord offered peace,
and so we went to distant hold.
My Lord was tested 'gainst three knights.
He proved the better, and most bold.

And so the pact was won, and then
much revelry did crown that hour.
Then he saw her, and his heart
went thumping like a hunted hare!

Soft goes the drummin' on the moor.

He walked with her in hedgerow maze,
to seek the fairest rose of all.
By her side none could compare,
and she bade him let no petal fall.

For such things fade, and die too quick.
If left, she'd see them year by year,
and close her eyes, where breezes sigh.
Twas then, he knew him, lost to her.

Soft goes the drummin' on the moor.

Then joined they were, and on they came,
to mighty keep, and fertile lands.
Her beauty took all in her gaze;
that ready smile, and gentle hands.

Contented did the people feel,
when their Lord Mared rode with her.
To village chief, or shepherd boy
each soul was soothed by their gentle words.

Soft goes the drummin' on the moor.

Around his tower, her roses grew.
To wander there was her delight,
and like a child, each rose she knew.
He'd simply smile from turrets height.

The servants all grinned, as they passed;
making a habit to go that way,
and linger in her lilting song,
to chase the deepest gloom away.

And none could hold a sinking heart,
in walls that seemed to hold such power.
Much brighter had the keep become
to banish any thought most dour.

Soft goes the drummin' on the moor.

Word came to him of rape, and slaughter
throughout the lands to south, and west.
Sword raised, or no - it didn't matter;
no mercy shown in the Reaver's quest.

And through each night alight by fire,
no living thing was spared the blade,
in death, and ash, and bodies scattered
ever northward to his glades.

And so, his word went out to all
with sword, and shield who did recall
the valor of their father's deeds.
In truth, they were defiant seed.

And they rose forth in desperate hour,
so swiftly gathered to the cause;
a thousand men - three warlord's power
and warriors who'd survived those hordes.

Soft goes the drummin' on the moor.

And so, in parting Mared kissed her
then bade her in those walls to stay,
and out they strode to the Fields of Ral;
so close, that's where the Reavers came.

And on a crest in lines they halted;
shield by shield, and hand to sword,
while to the south past grasses swaying
equal numbers stood, and stared.

A glowering horde in bright mail glinting;
prideful stance, and smoldering gaze.
No one moved, neath black birds circling,
set to feast, 'fore men reached graves.

And there, the one - the Reaver Lord,
Chingren did watch his gathering foe.
They wouldn't stand his Shadow Horde.
He'd drown them in the bog below.

And then what games of passion, and pain
in lands laid bare to Chingren's power
with sweet destruction wrought again
to all, except the mighty tower.

That, he would keep to call his own;
a seat from which to rule this realm,
and hang Lord Mared from its crown,
then drink ale from that fabled helm!
His gauntlet raised, and steed reined still
he'd launch his wolves among those sheep.
Twas then he froze, stayed by a vision
striking soulward - striking deep!

Heads turned, as forth the Lady rode
to join her Lord on silent crest
she kissed his cheek, to quell her fear.

Soft goes the drummin' on the moor.

With twisted grin Chingren did leer.
He'd kill, and cost Lord Mared dear,
and take his woman in his tower.

Soft goes the drummin' on the moor.

His Reavers set their gaze most dour;
their muscles tensed to murderous sting
to carry death upon that hour.

Soft goes the drummin' on the moor.

Chingren did raise his voice o'er all.

"Forth now my warriors! Make them pay!
For daring to stand against us here,
'tis ours, is all that they hold dear!"

"Now sweep them down into the moor!"

And so, they came in vicious rage,
like cracked ice bursting from towering peaks;
one ravenous cry for eagle's ears.

Soft goes the drummin' on the moor.

Each steady eye, it held the sun.
Each sturdy knee refused to bend.
No thought be spared to turn, and run;
no ground to those who crossed that land.

Then grasses shook, and turf did flinch,
as onward swept the howling wave.
And shadow came, as death's own wings,
to chill the blood, and make limbs weak.

Neath dusky helms, with blazing eyes
their shoulders dropped, as in they surged
to a shock of thunder, shield on shield,
as two lines curved, but neither merged.
Like two great serpents o'er the land;
no space to strike a fatal blow;
no room to bring down sword in hand
to rip the flesh of the hated foe.
Shields slid away, then blades came down;
for Clan, and Hearth the dalesmen stood
exchanging death where none would cower.
For all, they'd pay that price most dear.

Soft goes the drummin' on the moor.

But vicious men were Chingren's horde,
and slaughter was their game, and trade,
as corded muscles cut a swath
they grinned, as screams began to fade.
And on they came, o'er mangled husks,
where dreams of home all flowed away.
No more to feel their women warm;
no more to smile, as children play.
Yet, Dalesmen stood to stop cruel barbs
from finding friends, all moaning felled,
although that wall was edging back;
such was the crush, where the luckless fell.

Murmuring that the day was lost,
Mared's horsemen, restless stared.
One glance from him did quell those thoughts,
and then he turned his eyes to her.

"It's to the tower you must go.
Three warriors will ride with you.
The rest of us, will victory gain,
but raise the bridge, lest some pursue,
and I will soon come to the tower."

Soft goes the drummin' on the moor.

And with a kiss, he left her there.
Three warriors made her ride away.
He longed to linger in her sight,
but charged in hopes to win the day.

Forty horsemen on each side
flew headlong with a deafening cry,
with shields, and swords all forward reached;
all pushing thunder 'cross that field.

On Chingren's side, his horsemen stirred,
awaiting word to meet them all,
but they held to behold that voice,
for even they heard Mared's call.

"Now fly to save our valiant men!
Now fly to save a helpless realm!
We are the last 'tween hearth, and them,
and many souls, here to avenge."

"Now smash their lines with all your power!"

And forth they flew, to strike their line,
wherever the Reavers had cut through,
all leaving murder for a time,
to swarm around this danger new.
But, mighty men, these horsemen were
with flashing blades to left, and right
on swift beasts charging all around,
while death came like a lightning strike.
Fiercest of all, Lord Mared raged;
no shield, nor helm could stop his blows.
No seeking blade found man, or mount,
while crimson thunder stopped all those.

Twas then, the dark helmed riders came,
but fury was with Mared's knights.
More swift, and strong came countering blows,
as Reavers' thoughts were turned to flight.
The Dalesmen felt themselves renewed,
such was that valor close at hand,
and strike they did with wondrous strength,
while step, by step they gained back land.
And from the fight, so fierce above
more dusky horsemen hit the ground,
and though the Dark Horde did not run,
twas they, who knew they'd be cut down.

With every blow, a Reaver fell
so many there, avenged that way.
Free horses bucked, and bolted south,
and murderous hearts burst 'pon the blade.

And when the horde had dwindled down,
so many corpses, skyward gazed.
Lord Mared set to seeking out
the Reaver Lord, to test his blade.

'Tween piles of dead, he wound a path,
in calling Chingren's hated name.
Of all who spanned that bloody field,
no one could learn just what became

of the one, who brought a world of waste;
Lord Mared burned to make him pay!
Came word, he'd circled round the field,
to east, then north, and Mared reeled!

On the northern wood his wild eyes lingered,
to find the path his Lady rode.
Ruddy dust yet settled, in shade of leaves;
dread struck a bolt straight through his soul.

Then Lord, and beast sprang to the charge,
without a word, bound for the keep.
Few knights not needed to carry the day
spurred north, on each steeds waning speed.

Through shadow deep, and golden rays,
in silent wood, where nothing stirred;
it seemed so long to gain the glade,
then hearts sank at what they found there.

Five shadow riders had been felled;
all three young warriors, with them died.
With a dagger 'cross the Lady's throat
Chingren stood on the battlements high.

And Mared, in his saddle still,
tried not to shake, as up he stared.
Chingren kept his iron grip on her,
but she stood tall, so regal, fair.

"Reaver Lord,' brave Mared called,
'I'll spare what of your men I can,
and see you to your distant craft,
if she walks safely from your grasp."

Then Chingren sneered, "No barter here!
My men you'll spare, and something more!
Your keep, and woman shall be mine,
and fealty sworn by you, and yours!"

Those words did stagger all below,
for such a strength was Mared's bond.
Chingren had heard in distant realms,
no oath of his could be struck down.

And none could bear to break his vow,
so Chingren knew it through a smile.
This Lady fine, would he enjoy,
and all these lands, he'd hold in thrall.

She stared down into Mared's eyes,
in silent pleading not to bend.
Yet, a trace of tears was all he saw,
as a little more that blade dug in.

With shuddering breast, and glistening eye
he parted lips, to form that oath.
Instead, he loosed a terrible cry,
as she struck Chingren, and crouched low.

He tried to loose his grasp on her,
but fast she held him, as she lunged,
and o'er they fell, as Chingren screamed,
but from the lady, not a sound!

In headlong flight, awaiting death
her eyes held Mared's one last time,
as from his horse he leapt to run;
his voice like thunder in his mind.

And tears burned hot in wailing rage,
as bodies struck on moss, and stone.
To her, he flung his heaving frame.
She stared, but saw him not again.

He held her gently in his arms,
whispering words no one could hear,
and all back from that battle won
wept alone; no one came near.

Where the red sun fled, and the moon came o'er;
soft goes the drummin' on the moor.

He slowly raised her in his arms,
to place her where her roses grew;
on padded couch, in silver rays
where fragrant blossoms gathered dew.

We filled Chingren with thrusting blades
if just to vent our rage on him,
for ripping down that fairest flower
to ever grace our silent glen.

No more would he defile that place.
We dragged him far, there left for wolves,
then came to cleft the timber broad,
to see our dead raised to the clouds.

And many fine beds did we raise;
none greater than the Lady's pyre.
She'd lead them to those broad white gates,
and feast with them forevermore.

Soft goes the drummin' on the moor.

But little comfort did that bring
to our Lord shuffling in his haze.
The drums beat slow, and the sad Bard sang
of death, and courage, and a rose's blaze;

and a cherished reign from a fabled tower.
Soft goes the drummin' on the moor.

She lay high, where the song birds soar
on a bed of blossoms, thick with dew,
then when all pyres in flames did roar,
he took to saddle, and did not move;

but trembling, kept his eyes on her.
Soft goes the drummin' on the moor.

While he could not see her through those flames,
and when the timbers crumbled low,
still, he just stared where she'd lain,
til the sun took on a ruddy glow.

Then, he simply twitched his reins
to turn his horse for lands unknown,
and hire his sword on distant shores;
a somber horseman on his own.

And when death greets him, he'll be glad;
so I heard him whisper there.
He'll seek the fiercest battle mad,
til a kind blade sends his soul to her.

Far from a silent, crumbling tower;
soft goes the drummin' on the moor.

MARED'S HOPE

Oh woman will ye walk with me
where hedgerows hide the blazing rose,
and find that flame, and pluck it forth,
to pledge to you this wondrous oath.

A crown you'll wear, of hearts entwined,
to soar with me throughout the years,
to shine like starlight, evermore,
and cast away all care, and fear.

To dream with me, of many things;
a tower strong to light the way,
and bring our people from their knees,
to guide them to the light of day.

And sire a clan to grace the world
in peace, and power, and fertile fields;
oh woman, if you'll walk with me,
then all this could be real!

TROLL AND MAIDEN

Fangs, and claws in shadow ruled, and night, its armour well ensconced. Cruel bumps, and boils drove it on, sorely bound in knobby skin, taught, and oozing. Still, it was a quick, gregarious beast, with sharp ears twitching, in time with a short, twig like tail. Black eyes darted in flicking stabs, responding to the slightest sounds, but there was naught to fear in these woods. A slight chime of bells drew bone grey skin away from a speckled maw, in a horrendous mockery of a grin.

Setting a swift pace demanded an even more absurd angle of its bowed spine, crouching low, while claws raked damp soil. Brambles could not slow that loping gate, their nettles little affecting cold thick hide. Twigs ripped free, strands of hair, green as moss, set ink black in the night. Before long a cleared valley lay, like a blanket spreading away from where it lingered in the edge of cover.

Only the slightest hiss of frustration did it allow, finding no livestock in the outer pastures. Everything good to eat mulled about in high stone enclosures, each embracing their cottages, where golden light winked through portals, like stars across the expanse. Stone chimneys set a chalky glow, jutting out from rounded thatched roofs, all shimmering like golden helms in bright moonlight; a bad night for skulking! Smoke rose like so many lazy spectres, from nearly every chimney. The small folk were awake.

Not even a dog strayed near his trees; no easy pickings this night. It considered turning back, but the scent of plump cattle was strong, while hunger gnawed like a rat in its gut.

That was a distinct possibility considering the last meal. After a brief struggle at remembering it had chewed them all well, the creature gave it up with a shrug. A few moments more to consider, and it moved out into the open vale. One enclosure was near enough to hint at success, so swiftly it spanned low grasses.

Eadils sat with his chin in his palms, his eyes filled with the hypnotic dance of flames in hearth. Lost was he in visions to captivate a four year old boy. As a King he strode, with sceptre in hand, and all of his subjects faultlessly obeyed every command! It did not matter that they were kids, and calves; he was King, and he'd shake his willow switch at any dissidents.

The occasional grunting of his older brother, Cadagern, threatened to shake him from that kingdom, as did the resultant shadows of accompanying flailing, yet Eadils did not flinch. His rule was secure.

A bright blade hummed ominously, with every smooth curve slashed through warm air. Sparkling like the fire itself, that sword looked every bit as impressive as the young warrior who wielded it; at least in speed, but not so much in control. He had just well, and truly run some bitter enemy through, when a voice as smooth as the song of steel caused him to falter.

"Again, you wander too close to your brother."

To that, he made a face at his sister, who was seated nearby. She had the grace of a queen, but the humility of a milking maid; something he forever marvelled at, but never showed it. He set a defiant pose, announcing, "I am fully in control! At any rate, when else can I practice? I never have time in the day. I must become one with father's sword, or forever fight it. The burden has fallen to me, so don't you talk!"

"I am your elder,' she calmly countered, 'and the burden has fallen to me, to keep Eadils' ears firmly attached to the sides of his head."

Reluctantly, Cadagern moved off toward a spacious

corner, but not without some argument cast over his shoulder, "I am nearly a warrior's age. I do not really have to listen to you if I don't want to!"

To that Ythraine merely rolled her eyes a bit, then smiled, "Well, I am glad you do. I thank you".

He grunted, with a wag of his chin, while leaping about, and jabbing at this own shadow. " Well, sometimes I won't listen to you - it will do you good."

She smirked, "Spoken like a true warrior, but for now, you shall listen at bedtime.

He visibly sagged, despite some impressive flourishes, while that last thought even wrenched Eadils the unflappable from sweet visions. The child's howling protest was only quelled by her repeated answer, "Not yet, not yet".

"Shhh', came Cadagern's demand, `Quiet Now!"

He need not have said it twice as the livestock were clearly flustered. They could be heard crawling closer to the back door, bumping the cottage walls, as if they were trying to jostle their way through. Suddenly, a great wailing arose among the cattle, while bleating of sheep sounded, like screams in their urgency.

"Grab your spear! No time to go around," he commanded, with a wild dash for the back door, where he nearly twisted the silver ring off, in wrenching it open. A moment later he was outside.

Some cattle near the gate were kicking, as all bodies slammed into one another in their attempt to escape. The sheep to the left were a frothing mass, spilling along their stone enclosure. Still, nothing else could be seen. More light spilled out, when Eadils opened shutters above; still nothing!

He set a silken tone, in an ancient elven command, which soothed the animals somewhat, as they opened a path between predator, and protector. There - near the far wall, the thing rose slightly, its' mouth, and chest a single splash of calves blood, oozing down in startling contrast to its' pale hide.

It growled a gurgling challenge, heaving the torn carcass up, and into the field beyond. Turning back, it crouched low, tensing for a sudden assault. The lad did not disappoint.

"Troll", Cadagern shouted toward the cottage.

That single word grew into his best war cry, as he sprang forward, with blade glimmering high. He closed the gap swiftly, his manner laying low any hint of the terror he felt. Indeed, his voice rang fiercely, to banish any paralysing shards still lingering in his mind.

The troll did not move, but simply grinned in an eerie, welcoming way. Its' arms were held so low, as if allowing decapitation. Young men at arms would see the chance; experienced warriors would have seen the trap.

As soon as range was reached, Cadagern launched a sizzling blow for the neck, but all too quickly that horrible visage was below his blades' path! A boulder of a fist smashed into his ribs, knocking the warrior off of his feet. The thing was on him, but had to leap back, clutching its' hand. The troll glowered at Cadagern, then seemed to forget the dark, oozing slash across the palm. Again, it stretched the wounded hand forward, only to pull it back when the young man struck. Another trap it was, as the trolls' good hand followed that whispering blade, to seize, and nearly crush a yet slender wrist. Against all effort, his fathers' sword fell to the ground.

With a howl of triumph the monster slammed him into cruel, unyielding stone, grinning at the crackling sound, which signalled the end of this combat. With a gasp, and a ragged sigh, his prey slid down the wall, and out of consciousness. The troll raised its' fist for a final crushing blow, when a searing pain hammered through its' shoulder. It roared at a black, and watchful sky, turning when the blade was wrenched free.

There stood the maiden, her spear tip coming away with the dark slick of his blood. She shrieked a challenge, even more loudly than the screams of that boy high in the cottage.

The thing moved; she thrust, only to have the tip twist away in its good left hand. As tightly as she gripped, the shaft ripped free, just after her feet left the ground. An instant later it rattled against her head, sweeping her mind from the cares of the moment, as she slammed into billowing dust.

The troll ignored that wailing thing at the shutters, for time was running short, as evidenced by emerging torchlight reflecting upon a nearby roof. It hoisted her with little trouble scaling the wall with ease, before pulling her down atop its' stinging shoulder. The good arm cradled its' prize against ribs, and hip, and off it trotted, claws digging in, to propel it from the shouting, and confusion of an emerging settlement.

It was nearly black, when her eyes blinked open, only to close from the sting, and pressure near her left ear. Somewhere close by she heard the ripping of flesh, and snapping of bone. All the while, the creature kept heaving breath through its' nostrils, in a ravenous devouring. A sudden pause made her skin crawl, for she knew it was watching. Was it reaching for her? Would a claw come through shadow? She tried not to move, though she seemed to sway in rhythm to the pounding in her chest. Would she scream? Would she run? Would she die?

That horrid sound resumed, to banish tormenting silence. Her relief came as well from the darkness, masking what would have been a grisly sight. Still, the stench of blood assailed her, to which she could not help but gag, while her stomach rebelled. To that the monster chuckled in a low, guttural bark, leaning close to smother her in its stink. She lost all control! Her retching drew howling laughter; her sobs had it positively cheering!

Eventually, it seemed to lose interest, moving off around a corner of some sort. She caught its movement, and disappearance in the slightest trace of starlight, but darkness held her captive. Everything was a blur, as her night vision was seriously impaired by the pounding agony in her skull.

She forced her eyes to stay open, as she glanced about for any other source of light, but nothing revealed itself. Dizziness ripped her again from wakeful concerns. Her head fell back onto dirt, and everything was gone.

Daylight tormented Ythraine, even far back in the cave, where it sufficiently illuminated the mutilated calf. Nausea took her again, even after she had turned away. Her effort to shut the vision out of her mind, was aided by the equally shocking sight of bones, and skulls strewn about the small chamber. A chill seized her in recognition of a few humanoid remains. Her response drew faint laughter from further back, where shadow clung.

She saw it; two dark eyes peering from behind large boulders, its gnarled skull, a grey smudge in the gloom. She struggled to her feet in an effort to flee, but it moved swiftly to block her exit. She did not move. To retreat might invite pursuit, while any advance could bring an attack. Its eyes, like two coal pits, could not be fathomed, while its grin held promises of death.

She brought herself up to her best bearing, to defeat every trembling muscle. It took everything to keep her voice even with the words, "You would be wise to release me!"

A mirthless chuckle rumbled deep within its chest, to kindle menace in an icy glare. A slow purposeful growl preceded a step forward to freeze her blood, as she braced herself.

"That is just the thing. Kill me, and you will be sorry, you reeking pile of worm ridden dung."

"Hah! Elf flesh sweeter than Human, and the bitter Dwarf. Some Elf smell in you. I eat well soon!"

Its answer shocked her, though she tried to conceal it, forging on to stifle fear. "So, it speaks! I have heard that Trolls can speak..."

"I have heard that Trolls can speak", it grinned in an excellent mimicry of her voice.

This time she could not conceal her amazement. His laughter cut into her soul! He nodded, "Your brother comes looking for you; your voice leads him to my fangs! Hah!"

"No! You need not kill! Our Warlord might let you go free, if I speak to him."

"Warlord", it glowered, leaning into a lurch, but checking itself. "Which Warlord?"

"Pellerin is his name..."

"Pellerin,' he raged, slamming his fist into the cave wall, 'Pellerin!"

Not minding his own bleeding knuckles he surged toward her, but coming up just short, his eyes boring into her soul; breath turning her guts. His heaving chest brought the words grating through gritted teeth, "Pellerin! Filthy Pellerin - fool! What be he to you?"

She thought the strain to utter even a single word would topple her, yet she spoke, as steadily as possible, "Nothing."

She saw the kindling of those eyes, whether mirth, or venom she could not tell. Not even a cackling revealed his thoughts.

"Nothing! Far away is his castle. Why be he here? Why he comes after a milking maid?"

"He cares for all the people of our settlement, as well as his kingdom. He considers all to be kin, and clan. He protects everyone - even a milking maid!"

Her words had come on in one uncontrollable stream, lest her voice squeak, and fade.

"You are close to him?"

A chill danced upon her arms, and in her mind, as a terrible sense of foreboding kept her cautious. "I am - as you said. Just a farming girl, but word will have spread of a troll in the settlement. He won't allow that. You know that. His warriors are swift in the hunt, as I am told. I may be your only chance for freedom."

He tilted his head in scowling at her, and she knew she had him thinking. His quick glance toward daylight, brought hope however faint. Suddenly, he snapped his attention back to her.

"Hunter you say, humph! Bring the hissing death, he will. Hunter, hah! Maybe I get his hunters. Maybe I throw him dead at your feet! Do not run. I'll watch!"

He darted from the place, in a surprisingly swift pace for his loping stride. "Yes,' she whispered, 'you seek him. His archers will finish you. They'll pay you back for my brothers' pain!"

She thought she heard the troll chuckle somewhere outside, but little else stirred, save the pounding in her ears from anguish, pain, and rage. A twinge of nausea caused her to check herself, then seek cold stone for support. Bones strewn about the dirt caused her to stumble a bit, yet she kept herself upright, gratefully finding a clammy wall. After a few deep breaths, she cupped her right hand to her temple, in an effort to keep daylight from hindering her night vision.

He was watching the main entrance, that she knew, but if there were a back way; some passage too small for his bulk to explore, then there was hope. First inspection showed imagination to be kinder than reality, as dark recesses offered no outlet. She moved to see around the jutting stone, behind which the troll had been, but solid rock, grey in the gloom, and unbroken, dashed all hope. The cave was a perfect snare!

As a fortress upon a desolate plain, so too those boulders welcomed a desperate lunge toward refuge, however scant. Still hoping for some fissure hidden there, her headlong flight had her suddenly stumbling over two large forms sprawled across the soil. A third massive being sat reclining against stone, but the face drooped toward the dirt, as if no notice was taken. Even elven sight took some time to discern shapes here, yet soon she knew they were quite dead. Lighter in hue than either wall, or soil, she realized they were nothing but bone. Her eyes picked out the gnarled skulls, and misshapen bones of three trolls.

From the mouth of its trap, she heard claws rake soil, as it came raging round that monolith, and at her in a heartbeat. Bellowing confounded her, as its sweeping movement grasped a wrist to the point of breaking, hurling her to scatter bone. Some barren ribs brought a searing gash low upon her right side, so that she had to cry out.

She came to a stop in a crouch, casting venomous glaring his way, but the beast took no notice of her. It dropped to one knee where she had been, to move an outstretched palm above the still, and silent forms. At length, the troll grunted satisfaction, "Not mad. Not moved."

Yet, the gaze it bent upon her was vicious! It arose like a massive shadow in the gloom. Those eyes somehow stood out, to cast dark thoughts right through her. Claws scraped a slow, menacing stride, each thump of a heel striking another agonizing moment from her life. It pointed her to her waking place, and she tried to obeyed, but it kept coming to glower over her.

Its claw swept up behind to wrench her head back, exposing her throat. She tried to lash out with her own nails, but it clamped a huge hand upon hers, until her fingers were ready to snap! Still she sought its spear wound with her free fist, but the troll mocked her with laughter, which turned to a howling of fury, as its fangs came down for her throat. She tried to scream, but could not, even though there was no searing pain, nor rending force; it had not touched her at all.

Hot breath struck there in bursts, as it chuckled, "You need this, I think? Belly full, but this little morsel nothing to swallow down. Smell its sweetness! Touch it - I will! Leave it; I will not eat, till the belly grumble."

She said not a word, but nodded slightly, while trying to swallow. Finally it released her, sniggering, as she collapsed in sobbing. Ythraine wiped at her throat, until the warm, sticky feeling was gone. Cradling her aching hand, she gathered herself, to draw strength, and stand proudly. In defiance she glowered back, "You will need me!"

To that he laughed, "No - why?"

"To get you away from here. They shall find you here. You could reach the lands of men, where Lord Pellerin has no hold. You know the journey is not long. My father was of those lands. I know the way, and can be your shield."

"Shield', it echoed, allowing a smirk, 'no."

"Why", she pressed, 'it is madness to stay! You await death in this cave."

"Death - hissing death," the shadow grumbled. "You stay there."

She felt those dark eyes staring in the gloom. They stayed locked upon her for long moments. Its heaving breath subsided, with the tendrils of fading mist outside. He moved toward her; she tried to stand proudly. He simply brushed by, with a glance toward those dark recesses, as he approached the entrance to his cave. Pausing, he pointed to the place where she had lain. Almost in a whisper he commanded, "There!"

He waited till she moved to the spot. She perceived an amused smirk from the silhouette, which suddenly twisted an ear toward the outside world, darted forth, and was gone.

There she stood, swaying from the stink, and stress. Her lungs felt choked; she had to get out! Ythraine strained to listen for any click, or slash of claws on sod, but the cave walls played tricks with sound. Still, she thought its footsteps had faded sufficiently. She had her chance, but which was the best refuge? Out there, it would hunt her, unless she found the Warlords' party. A trust destroyed might forfeit her life, if it found her first. She considered a moment, then bracing herself, she forced a forward step.

Once more she paused to listen. Nothing could be heard. Ythraine was ready to move again, but had to look around the grisly place one last time. Every bone, and skull repulsed her, and yet her eyes were drawn, especially to the three dim forms behind that boulder. So much suffering grasped at her heart, so that she felt it breaking. She had to get out!

Birds went silent all around, but it was not that, which made tufts of fur bristle upon that gnarled hide. There had been a sound; a single metallic tone, like a chime swiftly silenced. There were hunters, and one had made that mistake. Not like elves to do that, nor would he have caught their scent, as the air was sweet with the fragrance of pine, and dew laden foliage. Yet there was something else. It came through slightly; the unmistakably harsh smell of man. The troll set a wicked grin. Perhaps this day would be his to enjoy!

It manoeuvred to a chosen area, where many knotted trunks, and moss laden stumps, seemed at first glance to be crouching giants; perhaps trolls. It liked to think so. The scent was stronger there. As awkward as its loping gate was, footsteps whispered over sod, in spite of long claws. Muscles stayed loose for stealth, although it stayed low. Ears swivelled for sound, rewarded by something ahead. For it all, he still knew the humans would be alerted, as the forest always went silent, when trolls were about. The troll slid between branches, edging up to dense brush, through which he peered.

There beyond, not far away, a warrior came edging along up out of a ravine. His sword was drawn, and trembling, as his eyes darted from one gloomy, misshapen stump after another. He had the dark hair prized as a trophy, by trolls throughout the elven worlds; humans being so rare. A partner of his also had the dark hair, but with a trace of red hue, when he passed through shafts of sunlight; less prized but still worth the admiration of many beyond the settlement. That one had a biting blade as well, but seemed much more steady. He would be a problem, but not before his friend lay dead, for he was too far away to interrupt the snap of a scrawny human neck.

The near man came on, straight to doom. He only paused a moment to regard the dense bush, before dismissing the obvious reservation showing in his eyes. The troll paused as well, running through all senses, and glancing about for any sign of danger. Nothing came; not the glint of a helm, the jostling of armour, not a whisper - nothing, save the scent of man, and he was there! The troll held its breath, until the man turned away, only to stiffen at suddenly smelling the creature it sought. Before it could turn back, those bushes erupted where the troll came on!

Furious howling froze the man in its tracks. The fool swung his sword, but only to have that wrist grasped, and surely crushed, if not for the thick metal band worn there. The man cried out, trying to fall back, as his friend came running so very far away. The troll chuckled, reaching for that neck; then came that sound - the hissing death!

A searing pain lit deep in his right side. The troll shrieked through pain, and rage, hurling the man away, as they came running, laughing - elves! Cursed elves, defying the senses, until they had him, but he would defy them. He thrust himself back toward that bush, when it came again; another biting agony, and another shaft sticking out of his back, causing him to stumble. Still, he made it, but only to catch a glimpse of another elf running to pace him on his right. That archer stopped to bring his bow up, and around in a blur. The arrow came true, but the troll ducked beneath it, only to receive another from left, and behind, in the small of his back. That knocked him forward, and on his knees, where another drove into his right shoulder.

The troll rose spinning, and howling a vicious war cry, as he closed on the nearest archer. The elf was rather startled, and young, trying to knock his next arrow, with the prospect of death bearing down upon him. The troll reached for him, but only the left arm would come up. Four arrows came hissing from behind the youth, to dig into the creatures' chest, and abdomen. Each great hunting head drove him back a step in succession. Pain made him delirious, while he felt his own body begin to betray him.

The youth launched his arrow, which ripped through below the right collar bone, while one from close to the left slid between ribs to take his breath. Muscles spasmed; both hands trembled, as he chocked through some silent words, before toppling amid wild cheers. Shafts protruding from his back snapped, with points driving deeper, as nearby bushes shook from the impact.

The elves ran forward, readying more arrows. Eight bowstrings drew back to loose down upon him, yet did not release when a man yelled, "Hold there!"

The dark haired warrior strode forth, rubbing his wrist, but still grasping his sword. Whether he blushed from rage, or embarrassment, no one guessed, all backing away at a wave of that blade. His companion came sprinting with urgent glances between the troll, and his brother, who scarcely paused for his apology. Indeed, the only thing to interrupt his pace toward his prey, was the voice of his host.

That resplendent fellow appeared from nearby foliage, every shade of green shining upon his hunting tunic. He brought a calm over all; such was his confident manner. A thrill sparkled within his eyes, only when he studied the troll, but quickly he left off the topic. Of his foul tempered guest he enquired, "How many trolls have you hunted?"

To that the man faltered, glancing about, "Well; not really - any my Warrior Lord."

"You should know sir,' the Warlord continued, without seeming to have heard, 'that before us lay a Troll, and as a rule a cunning brute. The ground holds some warriors, who have cast caution aside, for trolls can make fine corpses, until the unwary get too close. A troll will gladly take yet another life, so long as there is breath, and blood in the beast. Our arrows are by far the best method, and thereafter you may take any trophy; the head, a claw, or the entire carcass if you wish."

The warrior scowled a bit, then nodded. The Warlord grinned, turning to his archers, but before he could give them the command to approach, he saw her. She came from shadow, dishevelled, but still beautiful to him. Such was her grace, as to glide in a weaving path among the foliage. He drank in her every move, even noting how she tried to conceal her disapproval of the troll before her. Raising a narrowing gaze toward him, she said, "That is something, I do not believe I will wish to witness!"

All eyes turned toward her, most notably both humans, who gaped dumbfounded. The warrior with the bruised forearm, and matching ego recovered first. "I faced it alone. I deserve my final cut!"

In the countenance of every archer disapproval was cast, but no words, for these Princes were guests of their Warlord. That did not deter her in the slightest. "I recall my own brother doing the same, and without archers skulking about. He suffered far worse, and so, deserves more."

"With all due respect,' smiled the wounded prince, 'your brother is not here, and I doubt we can move this pleasant scene back to your settlement. At any rate, your brother will not be raising a sword, for quite a long time."

It was her turn to gape, as she gasped, "How is my brother? How fares he now?"

The Warlord strode forth to address her, while giving the troll a respectable distance. "Fear not my dear lady. Thanks to the elven blood of your line, his healing is swift. Broken bones, and all, he should be sprinting among those cattle of his, before our friend here stops rubbing his wrist."

Good natured laughter among those archers, brought even a reluctant smirk from the scowling mans' brother. Still, she kept the urgency. Somehow, she had to!

"I must see him myself! Please take me there now."

The Warlord regarded her a moment, then nodded, "Certainly; I can lead you out of sight of this, and the business will be quick, I assure you."

"No need for that, I assure you", she announced, sprinting forth to the troll, amid much protest, and tightening bowstrings, lest the thing spring up. Even the Warlord gasped, as she gave the carcass a thunderous kick, shouting, "That is for my brother! And your fine hospitality, you fool! I told you this moment would come!"

No movement came; the great bulk jiggling from such a blow, went like stone again. Nothing changed in the expression. Its wide eyed grimace stayed as a perfect mask of the agony it had endured. A bewildering warmth rushed into her heart, forcing her to continue. Ythraines' hands came to her hips in a defiant pose, as she trumpeted, "Ha! See here, could I have done that to a living troll?"

Absolute silence ruled the place, before the Warlord was the first to laugh uproariously. It took him some time to find control to speak. "Lady - dear lady - I knew you to be a gem among your peers, when first I laid eyes on you! Fortunate is the one who wins your heart! And yet, perhaps it is not you the troll wants."

"True,' she scowled, 'which is why I know he is well, and truly dead, for it is you, he wanted. Such was his rage, at the very mention of your name, that he nearly tore my throat out. Thus, if there was any life left in him, he would surely have been up, and at you long before now. His loathing would have cast aside concern for any number of archers, once he locked eyes upon you."

The Warlord Pellerin considered her information, with an uncertain glance toward the troll. His words were stifled, until his eyes shot a daunting glance in the direction of the cave. His countenance lit with a satisfied smirk, mirrored by the elder archers.

"Lady', he announced with an inclination of his golden

brow, 'we know well, you speak the truth; still, it would do no harm to test the bowstrings a bit?"

"Of greater importance to me, my lord, is the anxiety of my brethren. I wish to end their worry, as soon as possible, and tend to their needs. Such would be my gratitude, for this small favour, I would consider that place you have offered at Autumnal Feast."

The Warlord gaped, then caught himself, doing little to hide his pleasure, as he barked his command, "Archers to me! Give a place for our girl, you black hearts! And, a place for our honoured guests from across the waters!"

When all had assumed their places, he trumpeted, "Do not worry my dear. We'll soon have you back with your brothers!"

She wanted to look back, but did not dare. Instead, she let herself become distracted by the grumblings of the dark haired warrior beside her. She glanced, and he glowered, prompting her to ask, "Whatever is wrong?"

He gruffly replied, "All effort is wasted, because of you. I risked my life to draw it out of hiding, and what have I to show for it? Not an ear, nor a claw; no trophy at all!"

With a shrug she offered a sidelong glance. "And yet, there will be many trolls I think, for a warrior such as yourself. I hear there are many in the lands of men. You were brave to offer yourself in baiting him, but you do understand a sisters' anxiety for her brothers' wounds. I must also comfort the babe in my family. He'll likely not sleep for a very long time."

The warrior stayed silent for long moments. She could see his mind searching for an appropriate response, before he finally gave it up with a nod, "Of course; lady."

To that she smiled, "You are gracious sir, and I thank you for it. We have quite a distance to cover, I think, so if you don't mind, I would like to hear of your home."

Thus began a long conversation, all about a castle upon a mountain lake, and the peoples there. She had expected both brothers to join in that topic, but the dark haired warrior did most of the talking. Such was his assertive nature over the other, that she expected him to be the eldest. It turned out, the exact opposite was true, with the silent elder sibling simply being shy. Still, she found the man's smile, and manner captivating, while the few words he spoke, were delivered with rivetting grace. She tried not to dwell upon that.

The journey home brought nothing deadly, or different, but as they strode away from the last trees, a great multitude assembled, in both field, and stone rimmed lane. They thronged, so that Ythraine suspected many of them seizing the moment, to gain the notice of their Overlord. She paused to greet the ones she knew truly cared, but also accepted the embrace of all. It was a time for wounds to be ignored, as they tried not to look startled by her blood, and bruising. For her part, she did not wince, when tender spots were contacted, but rather held an indomitable bearing.

The archers cheered, all pointing at one another with nothing more deadly than an index finger. Pellerin the Warlord seemed to fill the area, without any effort at all. On they went toward her home, where human neighbours were truly affected by her battered appearance. Their concern brought a burning to her eyes, but still she summoned a dignity to be admired, which was mirrored by a youth she suddenly noticed directly ahead.

There stood Cadegern, with his right arm in a sling, himself trying not to cringe, whenever anyone bumped that side. He watched her for only a moment, before the muscles in his cheeks grew taught, and his gaze fell away.

Eadils made himself known in the crowd, releasing his grip on Cadegerns' little finger, as he ran to slam his cheek against her thigh. She picked him up, quivering from the effort. Eadils smiled, staring straight to her soul, as children often can, then embraced her, so that she nearly allowed herself to weep.

Instead she took the last steps forward, to nudge a shoulder against her brothers' healthy side. He did not respond at first, but at length cast her a bit of a scowl, to which she smiled, "I had best see to those wounds."

"It is nothing", he countered, yet still let her gently turn him into their gateway.

Inside their home she lowered Eadils to the floor. His protests died away soon enough, when he discovered glimpses of the hubbub outside, through various portals.

She soon discovered Cadegerns' right shoulder to be badly bruised, and his ribs wrapped in impressive fashion. He regarded their cauldron, hanging in the hearth, with intense concentration, while she uncovered the places where bone was fusing. She admired his resolve, as her fingertips tapped points of amber light upon those places. The orbs dimmed quickly; healing was well under way.

Neighbours appeared at the door to offer any assistance, to which she expressed gratitude, but respectfully declined. It took an adept bit of herding to get them all back out the door, but she managed it quickly enough. When she returned to Cadegern, he had not moved, while his eyes were closed as if asleep. Inspection of his back showed every bone in place, but still he seemed to wince a little at her touch. It had been a terrible wound, but no longer.

"This is the work of no village healer", she admired.

"The Warlord put his own healer to work."

"Did he now,' she smirked, running a forefinger along his spine in quite an authoritative manner, 'well then, I can add nothing to this, except to dress your wounds again."

He pointed out where the healer had left fresh linen, and let her set to work, but as she wrapped it round, and round, his breath became laboured. She saw pain flash in his eyes, and declared, "It is too tight."

He shook his head, then tried to keep her in his gaze. He faltered, staring back at the hearth. In a rush he whispered,

"I have failed you!"

She drew him into her embrace, and Cadegern wept.

Ythraine held him long, before she offered, "You tried your best. There is no failure in that! You fought well - I saw the troll toss a mighty warrior, as if the man were a leaf. It took all of Pellerins' archers to bring him down, and still they did not go near. You did not hesitate so!"

She could no longer defeat her own tears. Casting a glance about for Eadils, she quickly located him. He was busy trying to creep up on one of the stray cats, who usually found a way in. She brought her cheek back against Cadegerns' brow, to let their anguish burn for a long time. The evening passed that way, with even Eadils eventually joining in, until they were all too weary, and the revelling outside faded to memory.

Time began its healing chore, so that she was radiant at Autumnal Feast, having consented to be the guest of the warlord Pellerin. Even Cadegern could again stroll proudly among the maidens, although there was an agreeable difference in his manner. It was something she liked; a grace brought on by a touch of humility. Eadils of course, simply enjoyed, taking in all of the splendour of an elven feast. He especially liked the attention paid him, by the more quiet of the two princes from Maleath Dwyndir. The other directed most of his attention toward Ythraine, so that she felt like a hitching post between Prince, and Warlord.

The princes eventually returned to their homeland, and even Pellerin was drawn away on business of the Kingdom. Life returned to normal for most, but not her. So many times she cast the slightest glances toward those woods, while getting through the chores. At night she took up Eadils' habit of gazing out through opened shutters, in that direction. Sometimes Eadils thought he heard strange noises, like a cackling sound, dancing forth from the distant gloom of bark, and leaf. At such times he bent an ear toward his sisters' whisperings, and sometimes thought he heard her say something like, "Run you fool!"

SPILT MILK

Throughout the descent, milk splayed forth from a spinning plastic cup. All the while, the babe's eyes went huge, as she burbled, "Ooooh!"

The shrieking of her name, brought the tot's attention back to her mother, who scolded severely, while the cup clattered, and gushed across black tiles. When that tirade subsided, the woman turned away slowly, to fetch a mop. The toddler invested only a moment in gaping with patent, sad eyes, before grinning over her impressive creation.

The mop came out. The little girl displayed an expression full of concern - she was indeed learning fast! The woman couldn't be angry for long, for she was adorable in her eyes, and forever hers - for better, or worse!

Shaking her head, and grinning, she wagged a finger at the girl, then the mop arced downward, to glide closer, and closer toward that fine mess.

The tot stared down, with widening eyes, upon those pearly splashes. She babbled with wonderment inherent in all babes, beset with the glorious task of discovering a new world. And, the droplets did please her, all glittering in neon, until the mop would soon sweep them away. Yet, she'd enjoy them, while they lasted all drinking in light, and casting it back. They were riches enough, for one new to the world, as into spilt milk the journey began.

Down into one pearl; a single one standing, both tiny, and brilliant, far flung from its' vessel; the glare is engulfing - far reaching, and blinding, while the flight of a lightning bolt crawls to new depths.

Then speckles appear, as black as a pupil - the eyes of a spider coming on fast; expanding, creating a polka dot sea. Is here going there, or is there coming here, as a single spot brings on the void, and the glare drowns somewhere behind. Where in the world does the known world go, when the body meets nothing, and senses are tossed?

Pinpoints of light appear far ahead, slowly expanding; coming on faster, with matter enthroned. Swirling buds burst forth graceful in bloom, as onward they charge, birthing pure light - a garden embracing; filling the sky. Then down to one blossom of carnations' cream, the hornet flight settles near a soft petals' edge.

As a dark hue returns, round silent auld dew drops, each holding their spectrum near a golden heart blazing; the cool ones give way, and the warm spheres come greeting, to slide by beyond, and stay close behind.

Beyond a red marble, the blue one hangs waiting, then glides without veering, bestowing its' kiss.

And, into it's essence, through cloud, and light breezes, grand lands are revealed among ocean's bright gleaming.

Down to one land of jade forests, and wild froth, a stone waste survives, spreading itself wide in welcome, and there, stands a street, with a house of green panel. Its' grey roof fades to the sight of a kitchen, where there stands a man in an old shirt, and blue jeans, making a snack to power his day.

With tuna flakes smeared to his satisfaction, he reaches for mayo, with his eyes on the window, beyond which a goddess presides o'er her back yard; her clinging bikini revealing so much!

But, his forearm strikes something, which falls from the counter. With a gasp, his attention returns to the task, as his glass soundly shatters, upon that dark tile floor; spewing bright contents in a great swath around, while he barks some loud curses, still reaching for sponge, and towel.

Watching for shards he kneels ever slowly, bringing favored weapons forth, bearing down on his fine mess, where he'll end the next glorious reign of spilt milk.

ONE PHOTO

A crimson thread beyond the window spelled Charlie's victory. Somehow, the first rays of dawn had found a fissure, between low cloud, and the horizon, to spell his freedom. He couldn't help, but chuckle, as he finally allowed his head to lean back against a musty bedroom wall. One more glance against anything moving among those shadows had him convinced he was still alone. Only then, did he rub the sting from eyes rimmed red, by straining against the gloom, in those hours since his candles had flickered away.

No flashlights, or phones were allowed, and still he triumphed. Beams had creaked, and groaned, but no more than a hundred other buildings he'd known. Claws scratched floorboards somewhere above, throughout the night. More imaginative minds would have said rats, or worse, but he was certain of mice. Still, he had not ventured far from the bay window he'd climbed in, and not close enough for anything to reach in, and grab him.

For all the horrible stories of blood, phantoms, and terror told of this house, that was not a remote possibility. The Anderson home was legend in town, for haunting, and mutilation, and he was the first to enter in many decades. Headlong flight, sometime in the night was anticipated, even by him, but in truth, all had been quiet. In fact, it had been rather enjoyable. There had been no neighbors partying til all hours, or dogs barking at whatever intruder had taken to stalking his alley lately, and the lack of sirens was like a slice of heaven! In a way, he had found peace.

There had been one thing, however. When his candles had faded away, he scanned the sudden blackness as hard as he could, hoping his eyes would quickly adjust.

When scant detail finally emerged of the room, his eyes locked on something. Across that small bedroom, near the door, he noted a shadow deeper than the rest. More solid than any other shade, it seemed, where it crouched like a beast with massive shoulders, and broad head lowered, in watching him. The want, and dread of detecting claws, or fangs, fur, or flesh, or bone was automatic, but as his eyes adjusted, and details of the room increased, there was nothing.

A little later, when his nerves had thawed, and slackened, the thing appeared charging mongoose fast, and on him before he could move. His muscles jolted, while his mind realized the slumber that had taken him. Again, there was nothing, but he was certain his heartbeat shook the walls. Thereafter, he had no trouble staying awake, although all was peaceful.

And there they came; the first rays of daylight. He rolled swiftly to his knees, and stood, if only to test how quickly he could have moved, had anything really happened. Well satisfied, he swung his pack onto the sunken mattress, he'd dared not use all night. Pulling forth a camera, and tripod, Charlie set them up on the cabinet opposite its' foot. Careful to place it a little to the side of that tall, broad mirror, which crowned an expanse of unblemished dust, he made certain to aim his flash toward a moldy ceiling. It would not reflect in the silver glass he faced, nor go directly to his eyes, yet still, he knew he'd be blinded for a bit. The thought had him wishing the feeble dawn had done more to cut such suffocating gloom in the place, as even still, it was hard to see much.

He wanted to run, his quest achieved, but the doubters would be out in force, even questioning if he'd really stayed. This would remove the doubt, and so, he lingered. It was with a triumphant grin, he raised the trigger switch, and brought down his thumb. The shutter clicked, as the flash went off, and Charlie shrieked, his sanity flying away in a single crescendo.

They found him on the road near town. His fingernails had been scraped away in the monumental effort of dragging that prone form over miles of dirt, and pavement. His legs, it seemed, were useless, from deep, and terrible gashes down both thighs, and calves. Frequent spasms held him, while he swatted back against those ruined muscles, supposedly unaware of the agony, which must have dwelt there. He never looked back that way, but his eyes rolled vacant, and wild, as they passed over the horrified men around him. And the screaming, raking the nerves of every witness; it never stopped, until sedatives finally took hold.

A number of them could barely stand to look upon that broken creature, for they had sent him in harms way. As much to comfort their own minds, his transfer to the hospital was swift, where doctors said he could walk again, but they had to get 'Him' back first. They also said those wounds were not made by blades, or broken glass, but something a bit more dull.

Those involved in the bet covered the bill for his care, but stopped visiting , when it was clear he'd never recognize them again. No more bets were ever made, and no one went near the place, although there were short lived plans to go as an armed mob, and burn the house down. Concern over flushing out whatever had gotten Charlie put an end to that, with the final judgement being to leave well enough alone.

And so, through the years a camera sits, waiting upon its' tripod, just to one side of a mirror. Its' shutter switch hangs on a dark cord, dangling before a dust coated cabinet, and ready to be taken up for the next photo.

OLD GUARD ON THE WALL

When I was young the sea was home. Great glistening paths took us in trading of bronze. Weathered men we were who knew Poseidon. Fine times we had in his gentle care. But, his rage was swift with little reason, despite the black bulls slaughtered for him. Good, or bad all craft are equal, when he stirs the paths to froth.

On such a time the ship was writhing, as great waves struck, and threw the hull. The crew prayed hard to the mighty Earthshaker, for Pylos shores were within sight. Our pulls at oars were as hard as our prayers, while sea foam drenched us in Poseidon's fury. Through our strength, or his mercy dear Pylos came finally. Amid shrieking gales we made the beach with our strong keel striking hard in the sand.

Even the earth churned under our feet, or so it seemed for some time. Gladly, we entered the great city gates, where we scattered for favourite people, places, and mirth. Still ringing my ears I entered Red Bull Taverna. My home it was in gentle Pylos, when fortune swept me there. Dry, and warm enough it was, where many libations I planned to pour till Luna Passed over.

There, I saw a familiar face. A guard of the city the old man was. He was loyal to the sons of Nestor. Pylos prospered then under noble Thrasemedes. The Old Shepherd had left a great king in his son. But, it was Nestor the old guard spoke of more than his new masters. Both old ones had been at Troy long ago. With hearts bonded in all the fires of life from joy to grief; those old comrades were as brothers, even to Nestor's death.

Yet something was different about the old guard. A lonely detachment would often fall on him, while his eyes saw something no one else could. Rough lines in his face seemed deeper then, as if chiselled grim by some bitter Mason's hand. In this way I found him at that little taverna. Yet, something more was brought out by his wine that night. I saw tears streak his leathery cheeks. Their paths glittered to his chin till he saw me, and then failed to smile. When I sat down close by him he tottered, and stared, then told his confession in mild secret tone. "Let me speak of the burden I've carried so long". He began with voice cracking from anguish released. "It was after Troy fell when the prisoners were dealt with. I honoured an order high on Ilium's wall. Agamemnon's will, sealed the fate of a boy. To him I would be death's own hand. Little more than a babe was this Hector's son. I carried him up to where he would stand. There we looked far down upon those cruel stones, which he was destined to meet, upon that bright day. Then he turned to me, as if not sure what it all meant. Those cursed, innocent eyes I still see in my mind!

I reached forth my hand. He grasped it and smiled. If he'd hoped for compassion, he'd not find it in me. Still my heart did quiver, though many horrors of war had made it numb as the head of a spear. Sorrow found me, while I pushed the child over, and then waited or that terrible sound. The boy barely screamed through his headlong flight. Perhaps too proud; he was great Hector's son. The child showed his bearing, but death knows no master. With the dull crunch I knew; his spirit had fled.

Great Zeus! What some would do in war! I had joined the ranks of child killers. A cursed lot to be sure! Thick silence tormented, while I stood on the wall. Then music began there. It rose from below. A sweet witness it was of heavenly joy. I looked down to the rocks where the body lay battered. An eerie mist swirled all round the dead boy. As I watched, that mist took form. From it danced three figures; Man, Woman, and Child, flowing with those sweet sounds. Of a fog they were, but their faces were solid. I knew every one, though how I can't say.

First was Apollo glaring fiercely at me. Next danced kind Here with her eyes on the boy who swirled round his corpse, while up at me he stared. As the ghostly dance faded my senses returned, but its' vision burned brightly into my mind. While the long years passed by, that strange image faded. With the help of much wine my memory seems dull. It was long ago when Ilium burned, yet the weight of my shameful crime has not left my heart. At least I've told someone. I've that satisfaction; shocked as you might be, that I'd do such a thing".

He did not wait for my reaction. With a hand placed on my shoulder he hoisted himself up. With an awkward grin he offered a word of thanks, then my kindly friend staggered to his watch on the wall. I sat long in silence, till my flagon was drained. I thought I had known him, but not until then. Both kind, and cruel he had suddenly become. Twas then I took comfort with a favourite woman. I knew she would ease my mind.

When morning came with rosy fingers, I took leave of my woman to find my crew. A necklace I'd left her, which I'd gained in Delos. It was said to be of the spoils of Troy. As I walked to the gates of great Pylos the mighty, hectic words were exchanged along her vast streets.

A guard was found dead outside the wall. It was said he had fallen just before dawn. I rushed out of the gates to find the body. There lay the old guard dead on his side. The corpse lay open for ridicule. I alone noticed his expression of peace, for no one came near him; 'the foolish old drunkard'. Some said he often wandered too close to the edge. I also kept distance, but from something I'd seen. There, scarcely noticed, set all around him. The slightest trace of footsteps; a circle in the sand.

HEARTLESS

"Heartless? He called me heartless!" Brad chuckled, as he took a handkerchief to his stiletto. "He didn't even know me."

It was a hard plunge between the ribs, and a long path across the throat, which coated his steel. He wouldn't get it out from inside the handle. He guessed the blood of a dozen victims was mixed within, like trophies. "Notches on the revolver", he liked to think of it, as if he were an old time gunslinger. Yet, the Mediterranean had been his playground, since things got hot in Arizona, and this was Cairo.

Noises from the street were plentiful, even at that late hour, but over it all, he could hear a cooling wind. Whether it came from the sea, or desert, he didn't care. He liked the sound, and it even found him far back in that alley, where he'd marched his begging victim at knife point. The usual words came, of a woman, and children, forced to a whisper by the threat of death, then, and there. Compliance brought another minute of life, and no mercy in the end.

Looking down upon his handiwork, he laughed like a school boy, up to some prank. He always thought the sight of a man, or woman grinning below the chin was comical. Thus, his habit of doing it. Of course, the women lasted longer - much longer. He'd always gaze the longest upon their tear streaked faces, and exposed bodies. By contrast, this one was a well dressed older man. Brad needed the local currency, and that suit bespoke a man dripping in the stuff.

As usual, he was right, for the wallet, thick as the best

steak he'd ever eaten in Texas, yielded a huge wad of cash.
Quickly pocketing that atop his knife, everything else, went
down a nearby grate. He shunned the man's jewelry as
easily recognized, and so, with a genial wave, and a grin, he
set off on the quick, and easy route back to his hotel room.

Sunlight bathed his upper room, as the echoing song
of a nearby mosque, had him blinking away dreams of the
previous month in Monte Carlo. Brad wearily let curses pass
his lips, for he'd been again with Rachel. She'd wined him,
and dined him, let him lose piles of money at the casino, and
ultimately, never saw the blade coming. He killed her
quickly, because he'd had her so many times over the course
of three weeks, there simply was nothing left to take. With
the impending return of her husband from business in Asia,
it was time to move on. Yet, he would always remember
Rachel.

Rising reluctantly, he checked yet again that there
was no trace of blood on himself, or anything he owned.
Satisfied, he dressed, then headed down for food, and
coffee. It was a good hotel, where newspapers in many
languages could be had. Having selected the one most likely
to provide football scores, he began leafing through it, in
search of that information. All the while, however, he
noticed a rather dark mood in the room. Men, and women
in the employ of the hotel, were positively downcast, and
even the patrons shunned the usually robust conversation.

Finally, he tugged on the elbow of the young man
passing with the coffee cart. Automatically, the lad retrieved
his cup for refilling, at which point Brad asked, "Why is
everyone so down today? Yesterday, when I signed in, this
place was jumpin'."

After a brief pause, to keep his hand steady in
returning the full cup to the table, the youth struggled for

words, "The owner of this hotel - he is - dead - today. Robbed, and murdered."

"Oh, that's terrible,' came the killer's reply, 'and you have my condolences. I hope this doesn't sound inconsiderate, but I see the guests are affected too."

"Our boss was a great man; a friendly man. He would come through here everyday, shaking hands, and talking; making sure everyone liked their service. You'd have liked him, if you would have met him, but he was sick yesterday. He was only on the street last night, because today is our payday, and his tradition was to meet us with our pay packets at the start of our shift. This is usually a very happy day for us, but his wife said he was carrying our payroll, so the money would be here, incase he felt too sick to come in the morning. Excuse me sir - a woman wants coffee there."

Holding him up a moment longer, Brad asked, "Are you going to get paid?"

"I don't know sir", came the meek reply.

"Well, here's a good tip for you, boy." Brad reached into his bulging pocket, careful to peel off one bill, out of sight of prying eyes. He'd even checked the money for blood, and so, pulled out what he knew was equivalent to twenty dollars. The young man's eyes bulged.

"S-sir,' he stammered, 'that is too much!"

"Nonsense,' the murderer soothed, 'your story touches me, and it breaks my heart to know, the world we live in still has monsters."

Reluctantly, the lad accepted his offering, dipping his head, and thanking him many times, before remembering the parched, and aggravated lady in the corner. It was all Brad could do, to keep from laughing, as he gave up on the search for sports, to pay his bill, and hit the streets. In high spirits, he considered a pyramid tour, but was drawn into the magic confusion of a bazaar along the way.

The place was full of the expected wares for such a gathering. Everything from brass, to poultry adorned those stalls. The din of so many voices crying out the virtues of their offerings, and the hushed murmuring of deals being sought, and consummated, had his heart pounding. The sun shone brightly upon those same pale walls it had doubtless baked for a thousand years. Closer in, the brilliant fabric, and bleached paneling of so many stalls served to herd humanity into a broiling crush of life. Some vendors had places large enough to allow entry, for any who cared to browse, and their shade was welcome. Brad stepped gratefully into one of these, at which point he fingered a few necklaces, toying with, and then abandoning the idea of making one, or two disappear.

He knew he had the attention of the goods keeper, who tried not to really notice him. It was the way of the bazaar, that no one was ever long out of anyone else's sight. Brad likened the man to one of the pyramid guides, so severely weathered were his features. A smile at passing friends had deep fissures running off of his eyes, and outlining his cheeks. A full crown of white curls stood out like lightning, in contrast to a dark countenance.

That head did not turn, as Brad ventured further back into the stall. It was then his attention was drawn, to where a light breeze rustled a black shroud. Peeking underneath, he spied a clock, but not just any clock; this was a carven mahogany beauty! Claws held a clock face of great antiquity, and as the cloth was drawn back further, a face was revealed. Fangs rimmed a broad mouth, drawn back into a baleful grin. Eyes stretched to the temples for wicked effect, where they nearly touched horns curling from the sides of a shallow head.

The body was crouched, with one clawed foot forward, and melding at the hip with a broad brass stand. Yet, such was the skill of the carver, he wasn't sure if it did. The entire composition drew a single word, "Wicked!"

He carried it forward to the goods keeper, whose sudden scrutiny rankled him. Yet, his slaughter lust was sated, and so he ignored those probing eyes. Brad offered his most disarming smile, as he announced, "This little guy is great! How much do you want?"

Those bright curls shook vigorously, to the reply, No - please. It is a family heirloom. I cannot sell it."

Brad leaned close, positively oozing, "Come on; every man has his price. How about this?"

Peeling off a third of the of the money he'd lifted from his victim, he showed the man a full month's wages. Still, that head wagged to the negative, and so, Brad's humor ebbed. "Look old man! If I want something, I get it; one way, or the other. I think you've been around long enough, to know there's not much choice. Take the money, while I'm still offering it."

He drank in the satisfaction of watching hope fade in the goods keepers' eyes. The man visibly sagged, as his gaze dropped toward the money. With a sigh, he gathered in the offering, though not without a feeble protest. "Sir, there is no discouraging you. It is yours. But, I must tell you, that clock carries a curse. If your heart is not pure, the curse will carry over to you."

"No worries there", Brad smirked.

Again, the goods keeper sighed, "Then there is no dissuading you?"

It was the rogue's turn to shake his head, and so, the old one offered one last piece of advice. "I must tell you then

- a good thing. The clock will warn its owner of coming danger. It ticks more loudly, when harm may come to you."

Its new master positively beamed at that news, and no sooner had it been set, and wound, then two policemen appeared, at the end of the bazaar. The closer they came, the louder the ticking sounded. Once they'd passed, the beat subsided to the mellow pattern of a normal clock. The thief was ecstatic, with the exclamation, "Now this is something I can really use!"

The goods keeper said not a word, as Brad set off with his prize, bound for the hotel. Once in his room, he set it gingerly upon the mantlepiece. Welling with admiration, he declared, "Now, my little friend; looks like you, and me, are going to be life long pals!"

It simply grinned back, as always, but the ticking started to increase. There was no denying the change, and he suddenly breathed, "Cops!"

Returning to the door, he peered out, and sure enough, a pair of officers were questioning a lady, not far away. He couldn't help, but smile back at his prize, as he closed the door quietly. "This is going to be sweet!"

That ticking grew steadily louder still, and before long, there was a knock at his door. Knowing the topic, about to be presented to him, Brad effected the proper mood. The door was opened with the proper weight of spirit, surrounding murder, as the police offered the usual apology for disturbing him. "You know sir,' began one, as his partner watched, 'the owner of this hotel was murdered last night. Did you know the man?"

"No constable, I didn't,' Brad lamented, "but it's a tragedy, all the same. I wish I had. He sounded like a great man."

Both strangers seemed almost embarrassed to

continue, and at length, darted increasing glances toward the mantlepiece. By the time of their main enquiry, that stroking beat was positively menacing. "Sir, we must ask where you - where - sir, that clock is broken. It has to be. There's a man I know, who repairs them. He is just east of here, on the corner. The front wall is dark blue on the bottom, but mostly white, with a large central window. I suggest you take it to him."

"Thank you, I will - and what was the location again?"

Much distracted, the one officer elaborated, while his partner seemed anxious to leave. "It is a small shop sir, beside the laundry on the corner. It is easy to find, and if anyone can fix it for you, he can."

"I'll do just that, and thanks again."

"Good day to you sir," was their last offering, as on they went to descend the steps at the end of his hall. Brad watched them all the way, so trance like in their departure, and the entire experience had him busting a gut on the inside. Finally, as the echo of their footsteps died away, he felt secure in letting it out. Only when his wild laughter subsided, did he realize the clock had not let up, but rather increased. On top of that, a wind had picked up, though not a curtain stirred. Against that noise he yelled, "What are you doing? They're gone now!"

That brought a full blown hurricane, so loud, he had to stop up his ears. It all seemed to come from behind him, and so, he turned to face it, only to spin back swiftly at the raking of claws, charging across the floor. Terror seized him, as he screamed, and screamed; the agony, and horror, drowned out by the tempest.

All was peaceful within that room. Only the picking of the lock disturbed the stillness of a perfect summer's day.

The door opened, and meekly the goods keeper entered, carefully closing it behind him. Approaching, he cast a somber scrutiny down upon the corpse. Brad lay on his back, with terror frozen upon his features, while his clutching fingers, stilled by death, spanned a fist sized crater, ripped deep into his chest. His red shirt betrayed nothing of the bright color it had been, while flies gathered upon the slick.

"Dear, dear", was all the old man said, before turning toward the clock on the mantle. It thrummed, with a mellow beat. With practiced efficiency, he drew a rag, encrusted many times over. Gently, as a father with his child, he wiped both front claws, and dabbed at both corners of that grinning mouth. "Whatever will I do with you? Always calling the black hearts to you, if only to devour them. I suppose, since you only prey on the evil ones, I'm to consider this as good?"

Shaking his head again, the old one gently retrieved his charge, cradling it under his left armpit. "Now,' he pressed, in starting for the door, 'I trust you moved all of that money to their safe?"

He smiled at the wag of a head against his withered biceps, pausing only to acknowledge a squeaky wheel, on the maid's cart in the hall. "Poor girl will have a nasty shock, I'd say, but I suppose it can't be helped."

Altering course, he took quiet, careful steps toward the outer wall, beyond which waited a three story drop. Still muttering gentle admonishment of his companion, the goods keeper altered neither course, nor pace, but faded steadily, like rain upon a pane of glass, to vanish through solid paneling.

WHERE'S THE FIRE

The whine of a racing engine came thundering along the alley, yet no one stirred. Not a single head poked out of a window, nor did anyone show themselves upon the asphalt, in spite of the breakneck speed of this intruder. It was a simple cube van swinging into what may have been a back yard, had it been fenced, and there tires screeched on blacktop long since set in favor of grass. Once stopped, its rolling back door flew up, with two men jumping out, to reach back drawing fire extinguishers hung on the walls just inside.

One man was in full firefighting gear, while his partner wore worn, faded jeans, a torn tee shirt, and failing runners. A third party emerged, as the driver's side door flew open, producing a portly old gent. He shuffled, puffing air in his excitement, until he gained the back of the vehicle. In an old delivery man's uniform, worn to shining, he drew an urgent breath, "Right Darren. You know what to do. Way you go!"

Still checking the gauge of his extinguisher for pressure, the firefighter looked at no one, but hurried around the east side of the house, headed for the front. Watching him go with some admiration, the driver suddenly turned to the man left behind, "Okay Jim. Time to find the fire. It's in there somewhere. You must hurry!"

Scanning the place, Jim frowned, "There's no smoke.

It'd help if we saw smoke."

"It's there boy,' the man with 'Frank' on his label pressed urgently, 'you've got to go now! Up the back stairs!"

Jim started off a few paces, but couldn't help smiling back at the man he'd not seen for ages. It staggered him, that his father was nowhere to be seen. Reluctantly, he carried on up pitted cement steps, and into an old three story home of cream colored walls soiled over the years to a peach hue. Its steep black roof offered no issue of any swirling haze, nor any sign of trouble, where every window held curtains drawn to shut in perfect peace. It was his home; the old family home, and he held no surprise, when the back door swung readily open. Yet, upon this day, he felt strangely apart from it.

Entering the kitchen, dusty as usual, with the sheen of old appliances glowing dimly in the shade of that place, he saw nothing to alarm him. Not a trace of smoke came from anywhere. Passing through to glance into the livingroom with it's fuzzy ancient furniture, he still detected no trouble, nor could he smell any smoke. Visions, and whispers of names announced, and Christmas presents handed out before the hearth, had him smiling, but he forced himself to press on.

The next hall was the same, a scene of supreme solitude, where sunlight spilled in through panes lining the front alcove. He was about to inspect the back bedroom, when turning from the light, he saw it. On the stairs leading up, where shadows clung as if alive, a narrow tendril of haze traced its' path, thin as a serpent's tail down dull burgundy carpet toward him.

Not shying away in the slightest, he leapt up those steps, which doubled back to open on a dim passage

connecting more bedrooms. Still no flames showed
themselves, but there reclining feebly against a wall, was a
woman he'd not seen before. Her dark eyes barely opened
at the sound of his approach. She was a lean brunette, who's
short cropped hair fell to the collar from beneath a black
beret. Her feet were bare, and black slacks covered her to
the hip, but her naked torso was shrouded only by a navy
waste coat fastened by a single button. She tried to speak,
yet it seemed too much. He knelt close to gather her in his
arms, and get her out, but she suddenly raised a palm to
him. Shaking her head, she whispered, "You - you must
hurry! Put out the fire!"

He began to declare his concern for her safety, but
she repeated her order all the more urgently. As she left
consciousness, smoke slid from her mouth, and nostrils,
while her head sagged to the shoulder. He couldn't tell if
she was still breathing, but her words pounded in his mind,
"Hurry! Hurry! Hurry!"

He spun away taking in every familiar portal, which
had greeted him since childhood, but his eyes were drawn
to another place. At the third staircase, light shone round a
single door, waiting like a sentry atop that final, short
ascent. In spite of his great exertions, those few steps seemed
long, and his progress labored. At length, he gained the top,
and there, let his fingers hover close above the door knob. It
proved cool to the touch, and so, grasping it, he flung that
door open.

The room was massive, and bright, with a glass roof,
which seemed some seventy feet high. He couldn't quite
make out the far wall, also apparently of glass, as sunlight
bathed a huge congregation, all talking among themselves,
their voices melding to fill that space. The smack of the door

curbed their humor somewhat, and a few cast irritated glances his way. So many were so well dressed, that he felt rather awkward in his grubby gear. The fire extinguisher dangling from his right hand caused a few odd looks as well. A man with a tray of laden champaign glasses swung his burden off through the crowd, casting a disdainful glance back over his shoulder. As much as it bothered Jim, he had to press on. Glaring back at them, he shouted, "Where's the Fire!"

Mild laughter rumbled along their ranks, and many turned away, but one man looking rather sorry for it all stepped forward. "You do well to fear the fire. Yet, we cannot help you. If we laugh at anything, it is our own helplessness. Where's the fire? No one here knows, but you may find answers through that door."

He pointed to his right, where a glass door opened to an outside balcony. There was some smoke, but when Jim wondered aloud at the danger posed by a fire outside, the man simply shrugged, "It is the only place of any difference I can think of. I only know you must hurry now - more than ever!"

Not sure what else to do, Jim made for the door. It's handle was warm, but when he opened it, he was met with a cool breeze sweeping over that structure. Smoke came from a barbeque, at which two men tended the flame, and its' sizzling meat. The man farthest away left off his task, to cast a sorry gaze as he leaned on the rail. The closer one did little to hide his animosity toward the newcomer. Taking slow steps forward, he did not break a deadly glare. Still, Jim persisted, "I've been looking for the fire, but haven't found it. Can you guide me?"

Staring into those baleful eyes, he thought he

recognized those of the boy who was his nephew, yet this was a man. To his surprise, that manner softened considerably, as his apparent adversary asked, "Why didn't you try sooner? You can't find the fire now, because you are too late. Times are gone, and about to turn."

Helplessness washed through Jim causing his arms to hang to each side, as he pressed his back against the wall, and slid to the deck. Weakly he muttered, "What do I do now?"

The man leaned closer, in a rather more compassionate manner, gently easing the fire extinguisher from raw fingers. His voice came in a distant whisper, "I believe I understand now. You don't have to think about it. It will just happen."

Jim let his gaze slide away, to fill with swirling clouds, and dancing light.

The place was like a cave, with dripping water everywhere. Stinging smoke choked the hall, through which firemen swung flashlight beams in wild arcs, as they drew forth their burden, strapped to a stretcher. Suddenly, their pace slackened, as a muffled voice announced through its' respirator. "He's gone - he's gone. No use breaking our necks getting out of here. He hasn't been breathing since we found him."

Indeed, any haze on the plastic mask, which covered Jim's face, had long since faded, with no breath to cloud it. He seemed an image of serenity, where they drew him in a somber attitude, more befitting a funeral. Such was their faded hope.

Red light stroked through the entry hall, beyond which an ambulance waited. As they cleared the door, one of their number stepped aside to seat himself on a rail. There he stroked an inclined brow, giving in to his own sad, unknown thoughts. He nearly broke to mirror the tears of two boys, who reached through fence pickets, as they cried, "Uncle Jim", over and over. It was all they could do, as their own weeping mother held them fast to her.

"Oh man,' whispered one inspector to the other, 'that's the worst part of the job; dealing with the family. Those kids shouldn't see this."

His partner nodded, adding, "This one's that little bit worse. She's the widow of a firefighter. Her husband used to work with our friend on the rail there. That is, until about four years ago, when a warehouse collapsed. He was also the brother of our guy on the stretcher. It wasn't long after that collapse, their Dad died, like he just couldn't take the loss. So, we're carrying out the last of the line, except for the lady, and those kids."

The door atop the third staircase shone like a white cloud, the frame clear like air itself, setting that portal apart from dingy walls. Jim stood before it, smirking at the realization that in his waking life, the house held no such place. He shuddered at the chill of the handle, but it swiftly warmed to his grip. That door gave readily, seeming to vanish, as it opened. And there beyond, lay the great glass chamber.

As Jim stepped forward, the buzz of so many voices eased, while everyone turned smiling to nod a greeting to him. Even the man who had drawn away with the champagne stepped forth smiling, as he swung his offering gracefully forward, with one simple word, "Welcome."

In his first sip from the glass, he recognized them all, though many he'd never met. Most were family who'd gone before, joined by a few friends he'd lost too soon in life. It was a natural progression, as the crowd moved about him, like great arms drawing him in. Every handshake brought him closer to the center, at which point his father, and brother waited beside the radiant young woman, who had died giving him birth. She matched his age, but called him, "Son", smiling sweetly in tender embrace, and he felt warm, and glad within her gaze.

His brother gave him a playful jab on the shoulder, and his father beamed, "Welcome home Jimmy!"

At that, the old man grasped the hand of his Theresa, who saw only the rambunctious youth she'd married, as tears seemed to well in her soft brown eyes. Jim raised his glass, and took a sip, with many around following suit. He basked in a peace he'd long hoped for, within the sound of his own voice whispering across his mind, "Yes. I am home."

DIG

Chuck had to keep his hand above his head, like a shock absorber. It was the only thing between himself, and the roof of the pick up, with little chance of the one avoiding the other. Even in his seat belt, he was sure there would be lumps.

John just laughed, and chatted to the bad road ahead, little noticing the discomfort of his student. That is of course, until Chuck called over the noise of engine, and churning wheels, "How far is this bloody place?"

With a quick glance John declared, "First rule kid. Archeology is seldom convenient!"

Noting the scathing look from his charge, he continued, "Hey, Chuck. I know you're made of sterner stuff than this. That's why I chose you for this dig. It's not far."

"Yah, well, The shocks are gonna' break." the lad cringed.

"Hah! Not this baby', John laughed, 'she's been over worse stuff than this!"

Stifling a moan of despair, Chuck shook his head before smirking, "We won't be able to drink the beer all weekend, being shaken like that."

John cast an urgent glance, and then a smirk of his own, "What an academic insight you have."

The truck slowed to a sane speed, allowing the passenger to lower his aching arms, "So, how much searching will we do this time?"

"This one's easier. We have the foundation of a cabin to lay a grid in. But there's a special request concerning the area around it. We'll need some exploratory trenches; not wide, but they could go six feet deep. With the river so close, I'd doubt it though. I'll show ya' when we get there.

The guy who owns the property will be waiting to take us in. Kind of a grumpy old guy - real quiet, but I'm doing him a favor."

The river came into view, tracing a lazy path across its broad low valley, to the eastern range. That entire expanse stood much as it had in pioneer times. Farms were evident in the distance, but nearby the land was wild. They swiftly descended to where thick stands of birch, and yew blocked their view of those creeping waters. There, at roads end, a tall lean figure set his scant weight against a dilapidated gate.

John set a more respectable speed, so as not to startle the man, who took more interest in the passenger, at which he glared. Noting that, John was hasty to make introductions, even as he brought the truck to a halt. "Hey Edgar! I brought my best student to find them."

Chuck looked amazed, as he whispered, "Best student?"

"Humor him', John urged, drawing a scowl from Chuck, so that his teacher laughed, 'okay, you're damned good."

That drew a weak grunt of acceptance, causing John to chuckle again, as both stepped out of the vehicle. The old man shook his shoulders loose of the gate post, to step forward. John offered his hand; Edgar looked, and then shook it. Glancing a little too much toward Chuck, and none too kindly, he muttered, "Follow me in."

Crossing to an old grey pick up of his own, he didn't look back, but sped through the open gate. John, and Chuck both jumped back in, the latter instinctively raising one arm. He wasn't exactly at ease, as dust flew, and his professor grinned, but the dirt track through long grasses proved quite smooth. Soon they were near the river bank, where John became like an excited boy, upon sighting the cabin foundation. Pulling up near it, he shut off the engine, and stepped swiftly out, with Chuck following suit.

Edgar did not leave his vehicle, but leaned out to wish the teacher luck. His attitude toward the newcomer hadn't changed, so John stepped close to his client, whispering, "What is it that bugs you about my student?"

Edgar shifted his scrutiny back against the lad, as he sniffed, "He's got red hair. Don't much like people with red hair."

The professor shook his head, with a bemused smile, "That's it? You used to have red hair. I can see it in your eyebrows."

For a moment Edgar glared, but then he shrugged, "Just don't like 'em."

With that, the old man nodded once, then left on tracks of dust. John waited to offer a friendly wave, just before the truck was lost to view. The gesture was not returned. He then turned back, to make haste, as both tents were set up, and a fire pit dug, for daylight was on the wane. Last came two lawn chairs, beer, and the drive through burgers they'd picked up to kick off their first night on the job. Both men munched contentedly, as they glanced about like a couple of idiots, in silent witness to the beauty of the place. It all vanished, as the night took hold, and John's voice sounded, "Tactical note: campfires every night!"

Clouds took the valley, raising specters which danced over silent waters. Yet warmth still hung heavy there, and the sun, a perfect orb guarded the sky against all comers.

Crawling from his pup tent, Chuck thought he could touch it, and then blinking in disbelief, he noticed John laboring over his half completed grid. He'd started at the floor before the chimney, drawing his web steadily, until he'd passed the doorway.

The lad drew a warm rush of blood from shoulders to fists, as he stretched, and grimaced, "When did you get up?"

"That's why I've got my own tent man. I can come, and go as I please. Got up with the sunrise", he grinned, swinging loops around a peg.

"What sun', Chuck mumbled, blinking around, 'what's there to eat?"

"Man, I don't know! I packed sandwiches, and donuts, and cheese, and stuff. It's all in a cooler. Go find it in the truck."

"Looks like I'll be missing setting up the graph; sorry." He offered, but his teacher hadn't lost a bit of his humor, grinning in a way, which had Chuck worried. Sure enough.....

"You won't be sorry for long. There are trenches to dig, and layering on this floor, but the trenches are your babies. I want one across this side of that big chestnut tree near the river, and I haven't decided where the other one should go."

Chuck glanced around apprehensively, "What are the trenches for?"

John didn't look up, as he drew his string to the next peg, and casually announced, "Bodies".

"Coming, or going", Chuck smirked.

John laughed, straightening up, as he ran a hand through thick brown hair. "Well, this time neither. I get to study the site, and he gets some ancestors back. Seems time lost track of where they are buried. A flood wiped away the cabin walls, and the headstones, way back before Edgar was born. The headstones were recovered during a recent drought, just stuck in the riverbed down there a ways. Edgar cleaned 'em up, and wants to put them back in place. When we find 'ol Frank, and Helen, we'll note the artifacts on them, and replace the soil. Then, we move the headstones for him, and put them where they belong."

His student scanned the ground around, as if looking for a lost coin. Finally, he pointed just in front of his feet. "I think the second trench should be here."

John put hands to hips, as he considered the location. "Right in front of our tents. Hmm."

The lad lost any confidence, "Is that a reckless choice? Where's a better place?"

His teacher just grinned, "Listen kid; archeology is as much gut instinct, as it is study. Well, maybe not, but it's close. The golden rule is the best place to dig, is the place you've set up camp, because it's probably the same spot, the folks you're looking for would have chosen. Course that's for looking for dwelling places, but the bottom line is people don't change much through time; only their toys. This could be a logical second choice."

"So, you're saying we'll dig here?"

The smile faded from John's face. He let his head dangle to his chest, shaking it as he did so. If someone could groan, and chuckle at the same time, he managed it. "Just grab a shovel kid."

The trench across the inside of that tree was laid far enough away, so as not to effect the roots. It would have to be wide in that soil, lest it cave in, but the professor was an old hand at such things, having packed bracing. This would keep it shoulder width, and save Chuck some spade work. His student didn't slack off in the slightest, and by nightfall he was down to mud, at nearly six feet deep, in a trench twelve paces long. John left off his layering, mapping, and notes to scrutinize that massive effort. "Man, you've been busy! And it looks like my theory of graves under a tree are shot. I don't think you'll keep that pace tomorrow though. Lucky you , I brought ointment. I think of everything! How are your hands?"

Chuck took off his gloves to show his palms unaffected. "I've done heavy labor all of my life. I feel kind of guilty wearing gloves, but you insisted."

"Well, still; I don't need you getting blisters, wise guy. We'll get maybe half a foot more here, and then fill it in, but that fun comes tomorrow."

Chuck looked up, and down the floor of the trench, as if tempted to tackle that half a foot more, but John cut off the impulse. "Come on out of there kid. I'll cook us up some ham, and hash browns - maybe even an omelet if you want it."

Back they went to the tents, and truck, where John began rummaging around the cooler, and cursing under his breath. When asked what was wrong, he announced, "I had the bacon in the bottom of this corner, under the ice. Where the hell did it go?"

A quick look around him had the young man pointing to a rock near the fire pit, "There it is. You must have already brought it out."

John began to argue, but upon his approach, exclaimed, "Well, I'll be - um - skewered! I guess I did. Hope it hasn't thawed."

Upon grabbing the plastic, he nearly dropped it, "Oh jees! That's like it's still packed in ice! I must have just - no I - arrrr! Whatever! Chuck, how about grabbin' us some beer!"

His student set about to his duty with enthusiasm, trotting off to that same cooler. Upon leaning over it however, he suddenly looked around. His name had been

called. It came on a woman's voice, as if through the mist,
which was no longer there. He shivered with the sudden
sensation, that something was close, and watching; perhaps
right behind his shoulder. Yet, his eyes detected nothing,
and the feeling ebbed, and so, he grabbed two cans bound
for the fire pit. There, he said not a word to a learned man,
who might scoff.

Dinner passed with both men lost in their own quiet
contemplation, held in the flames, and crackling before
them. To Chucks' relief, John went to fetch the next round,
returning quickly, with his humor unaffected. After a time
of silence, he glanced toward his grid, then smiled toward
his student. "Tomorrow, you lay out your own excavation
site, the way you want it. If you find nothing, we'll pick a
third spot, and I'll help you with that. Either way, it'll be
'Chucks' trench'. The sooner we find them, the sooner I can
get you onto some practical experience in grid work."

After his day on that first trench, the bacon tasted
great - actually, everything did. In fact, it all went too fast.
He was soon of the opinion, that his teacher was a strong
proponent of rationing, even with regards to the beer. Three
was it for the night, but the lectures were unlimited,
especially when John swung into the ultimate application of
study, and gut instinct, the finding of Troy. It was second
nature for Chuck to take notes, but he had the feeling he'd
hear it all again, before the dig was over.

The crackling had died with the fire, where embers
cast a dim glow against their tent walls. In time, that too
faded, along with Chucks' hold on consciousness. He'd lain
still on his back, expecting to hear that voice calling him
again, but the wind had tired of playing among nearby
trees, and all was quiet. So complete was the silence, that it
was as if he could hear the stars themselves whispering to
each other. It mirrored something within himself, like the

buzz of a generator going too fast. Yet, even this slowed, and ebbed, to fade behind the constant of his own heartbeat. Then, he knew he lay, embraced by perfect peace, and he smiled at what the city could never provide.

Then, somewhere distant, John farted, and the entire thing fell away, but still Chuck laughed, "Oh, no!"

John just called out, "It's the dog."

To that, Chuck sounded incredulous, "I think the nearest one is twenty miles. If we can hear that; poor dog!"

"Are you calling me a liar?"

"Let's just say that dog don't cut cheese with me!"

"Fine, it was the Grizzly Bear, but I didn't want ta' scare ya'. Go to sleep, kid."

"Thank God you've got your own tent!"

"Yah, nothin' like home cooked muffins - sleep!"

Morning came swiftly, with Chuck unable to recall even one dream. More bacon saw breakfast, with some hash browns, and John mumbling something about going to get eggs from a local farmer. He also mentioned the man having a dog, and Chuck smiled. The last foot of the tree trench revealed only the water table, and so, they filled it in. At that point, his teacher left him, to have complete control over his dig.

As John labored on his graph, the young man imagined a line straight out of the doorway, intersected at a point four feet ahead of their tents. Having drawn his line, he didn't see his teachers' nod of approval, as he set into his spadework. The winding sun saw him down two feet, but digging more slowly than the day before. It was then, John stepped into the other end, to do his part. Three feet more had a spade hit what might have been an old dead root, not much more forgiving than the rocks they were getting used to. Yet, the scraping of a blade across it, revealed a flat surface, of about shoulder width. Sure enough, there was planking below them. John forced his spade down the side, as he pried dirt away, then let out a whoop of triumph, "Ha! It's a lid! We've got one! Gut instincts - I told ya! It's an easy bet they're buried side by side. I'll try a few feet over on my side, and you do the same that way. It shouldn't be far - the same level for sure."

Chuck began jabbing the soil a few feet away, where the sudden thud of wood sent a tingling through him. He couldn't resist an excited glance, which was returned. Their spadework was frantic, but the task seemed to take forever. At length, however, both lids saw the world again, and each shovel was laid on it's own pile of earth. Whipping a tape measure off of his belt, John handed it to his student, before pointing to ground level. "Okay, keep it up there, and hand me the end of the tape."

With that, John pulled it down to touch a coffin lid, "Okay, now put that two by four across above me, and we'll measure to the bottom of that. Later, we'll get the distance to the cabin, and I'll add these to the area map. Nothing fancy though; they aren't coming back with us. Oh, and my camera is behind the driver's seat. We'll need that."

With the numbers added to John's notebook, Chuck went to the truck. Opening the driver's side door, he stopped, looking around. There was nothing - he was quite alone, but his memory of the night before, sent shivers through him. He noted the passing of a squirrel in a nearby tree, before drawing out a tank of a camera. The only plastic on it was the grip for the focus ring. Holding the thing up to scrutiny, he wondered if it still worked. Finally, with a shrug he returned that prize to its' proud owner.

When he made his thoughts known, his professor agreed, "Ya', this thing's heard, 'Hey baby, what's your sign', more than once, but it's an old war horse. I dropped it, trying to make like a mountain goat, on the cliffs of the

Acropolis, and it never missed a beat. God knows what I was looking for. Gut instinct again, I guess."

Climbing out, he covered the proper angles with fresh film, before turning to Chuck, "Listen, these are your first dead folks. Sure, you handled the bones at college, but it's always different when they are first found. Some people think it's kind of spooky. I can remove the lids, and you can come around when you want to, but you have to get some cataloging under your belt."

His student looked into the nearest pit, "I signed on for everything. I'll get the crowbar."

John beamed with pride, "Now, how did I know you were going to say that?"

Chuck had his implement of destruction handy in no time, coming in from his side of the trench, he paused at the coffin he'd found. Looking down upon it, he asked, "Do we start with Helen?"

Glancing over, John arched a brow, "What makes you think that's Helen? This could be Helen."

The lad was a mask of confusion, as his eyes flashed between them both, "I - guess you're right. I - well, let's open yours first."

His teacher smirked, "This ain't Christmas you know. Okay, hand me the crowbar. I'll teach you to use one of those things like a surgical instrument; minimal disturbance to the site, and all - just watch."

True to his word, experience had the lid lifting with scarcely a scratch to the rim. As it was, the wood was all but rotted from years in moist soil, but the square headed nails had rusted to the point of giving little resistance. John slid his hand into the gap, while he handed the crowbar to Chuck, who visibly cringed, as a dozen scenes from old vampire movies flitted across his mind. His eyes lingered on that hand he expected to be grabbed at any time, and his professor read his thoughts. "It might as well be an old pile of rocks in there now, kid. Don't worry. Try to think of it that way, but show reverence for the life that was. That's the balancing act that'll have to become second nature, if you want this career. Ready?"

Chuck considered that guidance, then nodded. Gingerly, John raised the lid, straddling the vessel, as he walked its length. Chuck's eyes went wide, and he held his breath, as diffused sunlight burning through cloud lit upon bone, rotted fabric, and leather. Propping the lid against the end wall of that 'grave', John crossed his arms in assessment. "Well, I can do an analysis of the bones, but I'm guessing Helen didn't dress in knee high boots, pants, big ol' belt, and buckle, and extra large shirt. If she did, I admire what's left of her beard."

"Beard?" Chuck leaned forward, squinting, as he stretched his neck.

"Yep, black hairs across the collar, fairly evenly dispersed. What a woman!"

"Okay, okay', his student scowled, 'so this is Frank. Fine. Now onto Helen, right?"

"First, I snap some shots of this. Normally, I'll complete each one on its own, so there's no danger of the other being disturbed, before we get to it. But then, you're itching to get at her, though I don't think she'd be much of a looker by now. Let me get some pictures here, and return this lid. That's when we can get to her casket, but we'll have mapping, and cataloging to do on both. You won't escape the boring stuff while I'm around."

John pressed the shutter like a man possessed, kneeling close to mutter about the state of the man's health through life, and estimated age at death. Most sentences started with, "you can tell by this, or that", as if his hapless student was supposed to absorb it all. Still, Chuck knew his professor enough, to expect recaps, until he got it.

The man even took a photo of a name carved into the bottom of the coffin lid, 'George Baxter', guessing it to be the carpenter, and vowing to follow that lead. "If this guy kept some kind of business records, and I can find them, we might find out more about our happy couple. Edgar told me a fair bit, and I may find nothing anyway, but you have to cover everything.

The lid was placed back over its' coffin, whereupon John edged past Chuck with the words, "Okay, ready for Frank now?"

An incredulous scowl was met with a chuckle, as the crowbar was taken up. The lid came off in similar fashion, with each rusted nail giving little resistance. When it lifted, the lad drew back against the trench wall. Her head had been turned up, and to the left, at an angle which happened to look directly at him. He realized that the skull must have lain like that for ages, with himself just happening to pick the exact spot to intersect the gaze of empty sockets. Still, the tremors ran through him. He had started to feel cold, with the inspection of Frank, but on this second viewing, it was as if the winds had bypassed his clothing altogether.

There was no skin left on the face, but some hair lingered in wispy tendrils, long, and golden. The dress, in tatters showed bone, where it had rotted away. A string of pearls hung round her neck, strung through a thick gold band.

"Chuck', his professor's voice sounded distant at first, but seemed to slam his ears on second try, 'Chuck, listen. Go sit down."

A blank stare held the man, who was standing not far off, before a glance out of the trench, and toward their truck had the lad mumbling, "Look, I'm fine. I'll stay here."

His teacher stared for what could have ben an

eternity, then agreed, "Okay, but I cut this short for the day. A few photos, I close it up, and we get a fire going, alright?"

With the pictures snapped, and the cover back on, a fire wasn't long in building, and Chuck was glad of it's warmth. John didn't look much at him, but concentrated mostly on the flames. At length, he broke the silence, "You did alright, kid. On my first one, I was about the same, but I couldn't touch somebody's bones at all. And yet, we have some serious cataloging to do. Then, I have to go for a while."

An urgent glance from his student preceded, "For how long?"

John pondered that reaction, before smirking, "Don't sweat it, man. I'm stocking up on more supplies, calling Ariadne at the mammoth dig to see how things are going, and then following up on our carpenter. I'll probably have to stay in town over night."

"Great', Chuck groaned, 'you open up some coffins, and then you leave me here!"

John laughed, "Look, think of them as a couple of old logs. The leaves in the trees will move more than they will, so don't worry. This is archeology, man. I had to roll out my sleeping bag in the midst of a bunch of South American mummies once, and they still had their skin. Try writing a letter home, with some kid who's been dead for three thousand years looking over your shoulder."

Chuck said not a word, but threw a rock in the fire. John carried on unrelenting, "Did you check if that was an arrowhead first?"

The steely glare of his student had him laughing, but then he reasoned, "I know you wanted the mammoth dig, but you know what that is? The zoo tour! 'Everybody hold hands, and stay in line, and we'll all have a wonderful time.' Well, hell; I'll take you to the mammoth dig, when we're done here. But you know, this is the dig Ariadne would rather be on. She lives, and breaths these pioneer sites. Most people think the most exciting thing you'll find is a skillet, but those are the uneducated ones - the folks, who need a mammoth to hold their attention. Not that there's anything wrong with that."

Chuck didn't look up from the fire, as he grabbed a stick, mumbled about it not being an arrow shaft, and poked the embers. To that, John shook his head, "Look, do you know why you are here? Because you asked the great questions. You showed an inborn instinct for the craft, and I think you'll make a good Archeologist, if you want to pursue it. I get so many passing through my classroom, eating up valuable butt space, on what they think is an 'easy' elective, it's nice to be able to hand pick somebody, who can handle a dig on their own. This is the meat, and potatoes of my science, and you can handle it."

A smile slowly grew on his student's face. "You know you talk too much."

John looked dumbfounded, then broke into a chuckle, "That's what she keeps telling me! Well, I profess young man, I profess. That's why I'm the Professor."

"You're also way too happy," the lad smirked.

"Yah, well', John cast a narrowing glare, 'as my student, it's your job to sit down, and shut up."

Both men laughed, and set in to dinner, as the stars grew more brilliant above them. The sighing of a light breeze among shoreline trees calmed the soul, and then, too soon, it was time to retire to tents.

Chuck slept deeply, but amid strange dreams, of fire, and grey smoke belching to the sky; of arrows flying, and guns blasting, their terror bringing children to scream. And there was blood. A red stream flowed below, down an exposed thigh, shining in the sun, and covered someone laying still as a stump in the distance, where he had collapsed over the axle of his wagon. The arrows in his back caused a huge stain, which no longer spread.

Then Chuck looked earthward, to see a shadow; a woman's shadow, staggering, as blood pelted the ground beneath. That sod came up, and everything went black. He then thought he heard his name, and forced himself to wakefulness. That woman's distant voice was on him again, calling it seemed, from the river.

Forcing his eyes open, and peering that way, through an opening in his tent, he saw her. As if laying on her belly, on the very air, she hovered in a flowing gown. Her eyes never left him - silver eyes, for she was shimmering like the very moonlight. And white she was, with her long hair shining so, he knew it would flow golden, if she were of this world.

At first his heart jolted, yet terror fled from him, as her arms stretched forth in welcome, and she smiled so, that he couldn't help but feel that pounding in his chest grow warm. He thought she would fly in upon him, but she stayed distant, and he realized the woman hovered right over her grave.

As beautiful as she was, he blinked the dryness from his eyes, and upon focusing, he saw only mist. It had come up from the river, advancing slowly over those trenches. Soon, even they were obscured, and somehow, sleep found him again.

Something touched his leg; jabbed more like. It was John's boot, swung in to wake his student. "Come on. I've got to make tracks today, so let's get to it. Last of the bacon, and pancakes is on."

Chuck smelled it, and that was a power sufficient to draw him out. Yet, throwing cloths on quickly against the chill, he couldn't help but notice, "Man, it's pretty dark still.

What time is it?"

"Exactly the right time to get started of course', John countered, 'since time is my worry, when I go back to the real world. You can forget about time, but I'll be wanting grid work done when I'm gone, and you've seen me in action. So, pretend you're me."

"Okay then, I'll go to town", the lad grinned, and the look of warning he earned was priceless, as John silently pointed toward breakfast.

There scarcely seemed time to wolf it down, as his professor gulped coffee, and led the way. Back in the trench, John elected to work Helen's casket, declaring, "You seemed to have trouble with this, so let's get the tougher one done first."

Edging into the gap, Chuck made certain to stand at a different angle to the coffin. When the lid came up, he was much relieved not to be in the line of sight. John had cleared space on either side, so that kneeling to her left, he motioned Chuck opposite. "Okay, I'll sketch, and you check things out. We'll start with the head. There's not a lot of hair left, but imagine her wearing something in the back. The skull is tilted, as if something is back there. You should be able to see it from your side."

Craning his neck, and glancing sideways, Chuck announced, "Hey, you're right! There's something like silver back there."

"Okay, I'll need it carefully removed for one photo. I'll sketch from that, so we can put it back right away, exactly as it was. This will be a once over lightly, 'cause I have to make tracks.'"

Under a discerning eye, the hands of an apprentice fought off their trembling, as they reached down to cradle the skull, only to jerk back from contact. His mentor smiled, "Bloody cold, hey? Like I said before, think of it as a rock."

"But there are spiders in her mouth, man", the lad shuddered.

"Yeah, well', John shrugged, 'I've also said that bugs are not exactly the best part of it. They probably came in last night. Better here, than in your sleeping bag. So, now like, try not to snap the neck, okay?"

His charge cast an apprehensive glance, to which he shrugged, "Alright, so it's a fragile rock."

Steeling himself, Chuck slid the hair clasp free, while everything stayed intact. Basking in his well earned praise, he held it forth, beneath a hovering lens. The click of a shutter, signaled it's return. "Okay, we'll leave the pearls, and ring right where they are, and I'll get a close up."

John did exactly as he said, but requested a search by his student, on that band of gold, for any inscriptions. With hands still shaking a bit more than he would have liked, Chuck lifted the pearls enough to turn icy metal between his fingers. A complete rotation revealed nothing.
Setting it all back upon moist breast bone, he drew off to take a breath, shaking his head at John's enquiry if there was even a date.

Shrugging, John recovered a small piece of what had been a fine dress, using tweezers to place it in a plastic envelope. "We've got Edgar for dates, but if we had to, this could lock it right down. He told me she died when his grand father was a child, not even in school yet. That made the man an orphan, facing a very hard life. Anyway, I'll ask Edgar for any years, and stuff. Time to move on to Frank. I'll hammer down the lids for you, but don't fill in the graves. I'll have time to do good sketches when I get back."

Again Frank seemed easier by comparison; more like rocks with no reason to cradle the skull. Yet, checking pockets was a bit harrowing. Only a watch was found, in slimy material ready to crumble. Not surprisingly, some did, which led to the discovery of an arrowhead inside the rib cage. Chuck thought John had won a lottery for a second, but it's extraction was by the book, accompanied by another quick lecture. "Now, I'd call this, the cause of death, since it was close to where the heart would be anyway. Hmm, it didn't kill him right away - maybe not for quite some time. There's a bit of arrow shaft still attached, more stained from blood, than if it had killed him fast. Besides, see those slash marks on the two ribs there? The arrowhead could have made one of them, but not all. Somebody tried to dig the sucker out, but gave up. You can tell by the healing of the bone, that he carried the thing in him, maybe even for a year. This is great!"

More photos gave way to the hammering of lids, followed by a speedy overview of the cabin floor. After much nodding in apparent understanding, offered by the apprentice, the other felt secure enough to go. Leaving a smaller cooler stocked with dinner, breakfast, juice, and beer, John was off in a cloud of dust.

When the engine revs had subsided sufficiently, Chuck turned back, to survey his own new world. Somewhere upstream, breezes rustled distant leaves. It was as if he could hear the shimmering of the world, against clouds crowding an arching sun. He breathed deeply of the calm, which banished even the tinge of apprehension, which usually struck when his eyes crossed those graves. At least for that moment, his mind couldn't conjure a single dread thought. With some regret, he gave his surroundings one lingering look, before moving to center his attention on the grid.

Work went slowly, but smoothly, and he soon became used to maneuvering over strings marking off foot wide squares. The troweling, brushing, gathering, notations, and mapping kept his mind engaged, so that he

quite ignored the occasional sensation of being 'not alone'.
He only paused when the trees whispered his name - once.
Listening intently, Chuck shook off a sudden chill, by
finding refuge in the task before him.

Time came to set aside his tools, with the sinking of
the sun. Kindling flared, and dinner was made with little
sound. All the while, he drank in the tart smell of burning
wood, and watched that shining ribbon of water wind off
slowly toward a purple sky. The brew was smooth, as he
concentrated on a cool breeze, and waking stars. Too soon, it
all made his eyes heavy, and so, he retreated to his tent.

Rolling into his sleeping bag, chuck froze at the sight
of a hazy form standing at the threshold of the cabin. To his
relief, it proved to be river mist, swiftly torn asunder by a
puff of wind, and swept downstream. Again, the chill came,
lingering that little bit longer, as he desperately sought
sleep.

However long he'd managed to dream, he could not
tell, but the smell of fish frying in butter greeted his
emerging senses. Chuck's eyelids were red against warm
sunshine, and he had to shield his eyes to focus. Birds sang,
and bickered nearby, while chimney smoke wafted across
the yard. His body jolted at the unexpected sight of a cabin
standing, where the grid had been laid out.

Iron leaf hinges creaked, as bleached planks drew
back to open a portal in a thick log, and mud wall. No
spectral hand did the deed, but that of a woman who
stepped forth; the woman he'd seen wreathed in moonlight.
She stood in a frayed long dress of cream, and light blue
stripes, and black ankle high boots much scuffed by the
labors of a frontier widow.

He saw the mound, and lone cross near his tent. She
followed that glance, and tried not to look sad. Deflecting
such thoughts with a disarming smile, she announced,

"You'll never fix that fence laying there. Come on in for breakfast."

It seemed a full minute he gaped in silence, after she'd returned to the cabin's depths, obviously guarding against the burning of the fish. He heard the meat sizzle, and sniffed frying butter, and crackling wood. Above it all he let that voice sooth him, as she hummed some forgotten ballad, only breaking the solace to announce, "I'll not come to the door, until you are dressed. So, hurry please, and come to breakfast."

In those sights, and sounds of a forgotten world, he hurriedly complied. He soon stepped out among sun's rays, kindling so many cottonwood puffs shining in lazy swirls around him. Animals, apparently quite used to Chuck, offered scant scrutiny in their various pens. He smiled at piglets bouncing through tiny steps, as they tried to follow their mother around that enclosure. Their urgent passing annoyed a dozen chickens, who felt it best to cover at least a few steps toward the coup, clucking complaint, as they went.

Amid the birch nearby, four goats were allowed to roam free, ripping ample tufts of undergrowth. Upstream of them, he saw the fence ending nearly at the water, and remembered that a tree had fallen, taking down three sections. He was to cut it up for stove fuel, but also fashion what branches he could, into fence poles, as Frank had done. How he knew that, Chuck couldn't guess, but he was soon reaching tentatively, to touch a solid door frame, still cool before the sun found it.

"You must be a carpenter, the way you are so fascinated by that."

Her voice startled him a bit, but she was too busy applying tongs to boiling potatoes, to notice. It all smelled wonderful, and with his mind grasping desperately for any slight hold on reality, he decided to let his stomach lead him headlong, into this illusion. Sitting where she indicated with a quick wave of her hand, breakfast was before him in a heartbeat. Other than thanking her, he could only think of asking, "Do you fish as well?"

Helen laughed, but only a bit, before offering an embarrassed shrug, "I've tried, but have seldom had luck. I gave up long ago. The hooks have all but rusted away. There's a local Indian Chief about twenty miles downstream. He just started giving me things when..."

She decided to concentrate on the tea, but in time broke the silence. "He even trades for tea bags, and gives me some. They just refuse to let a widow go hungry."

Helen glanced at him, with a mist forming in those beautiful eyes. "Please excuse me. A year does not seem very long to me now. It is strange, but after the Oregon attacks, I thought all Indians would be out to kill us. This was the only direction we could run, but these people have been wonderful. Just wonderful!"

Thinking better of mentioning the arrowhead, Chuck offered, "I am sorry. I guess you miss him terribly"

She seemed struck for a moment, easing herself into a chair, "At times - not. That sounds horrible, but he was not - a gentle man."

Crossing arms against a chill, which caught only her, Helen rocked slightly, as she seemingly stared right through the wall standing between herself, and that silent grave. "Please forgive me, for I say too much, but it's more like we waded through hell together for a time. I wouldn't call it any more than that. It's a long way from Boston, after all."

Rising suddenly, she strode for the door. "Please just enjoy your breakfast. I'll bring water to the fence later. Please excuse me."

She vanished to daylight, as effectively as any

phantom, so that Chuck was certain the entire thing would fall away, but it didn't. Fresh trout, fried in butter was a delicacy he'd never known before. Though he couldn't shake the image of her goats, in wondering where the butter came from, he savored it all the same. The meal ended rather sooner than he would have liked, but as silently promised, Chuck stirred himself to the task at hand.

Emerging from the cabin, he saw eggs in a basket near the coup, and one of the goats being milked, which made him cringe a bit. He hoped for a flash of those blue eyes in passing, only to be disappointed, as her concentration was intense.

It was cool along dim pathways, below a brilliant canopy, but he knew that would change. Broad leaves lolling at the highest reaches, shone like stained glass in a cathedral, awakened by the coming sun. Chuck breathed deeply of the green.

The fence came to view soon enough, with it's felled section directly ahead. He could see three poles shattered by the impact, where the trunk still lay across them. Such a tangle were its' many branches, no large animal could have passed through in either direction. It had been worked on, however, as new posts were fashioned from some of the larger limbs, and laid to one side. He wondered if that had been him.

An axe had been sunk into the top of its' fallen body, and this, he wrenched free with the same fervor he'd shown with a spade. Though shade, and cool breezes held the place, he soon felt like he was burning up, as perspiration forced the removal of his shirt. The blade seldom stopped, where all branches came away from the trunk, which he then began to section. That's when she came. The water bucket must have weighed heavily, but she bore it well, only hesitating a little when she saw him. "Well, you have been busy", she grinned.

The bucket was set close, and the ladle drawn, which she presented to him with both hands, one finger gently touching below its' cup. The rim was to his lips, and the water felt wonderful. He let his eyes close in the sudden realization of how drained he had felt. Yet, she fared little better, having in fact, unbuttoned her dress to the breast bone, to cool her glistening skin. He knew her to be a humble woman of her time, but heavy work in sun baked sheds decreed it, and days alone had made it a habit.

He opened his eyes to let them linger upon her, but she bent her concentration to the water. Returning ladle to bucket, she asked, "Would you like more?"

Words would not come for a moment, until he managed a rather feeble assent. The ladle came forth, as before, but this time it was nearly dropped, as he let his fingers glide, feather light over hers. Once he accepted it for himself, she drew both hands back before her chest, rubbing them, as if they were burned. Still, she held a gracious smile, as he reached forth asking, "What about you?"

She looked away toward the bucket, but did not turn from him, as she almost whispered, "Perhaps later, thank you."

He drew a hand from the ladle, to reach forth, and trace another gentle path upon her skin, this time along the velvet of her far cheek, as he slowly turned that beautiful face toward him. Her eyes lingered over his own shimmering torso, settling with some urgency on the cup lowered by his side, where water was spilling. Almost in a gasp, she said, "The water! Don't waste it!"

He simply smiled, "Yes, don't waste it."

She then looked up into his eyes, to bathe his soul entirely in splendid blue. Helen seemed to lean forward as well, until a shock coursed through her body, as his hands slid to her ribs. So shyly did she draw away, he felt his heart melt even more.

"I must turn attention to dinner soon. The sun is in decline. One of the men up valley brought some cured sausage I can prepare. I've some cheese, which I only just made before you - I had best go."

Helen only paused to accept the ladle, with a quick, and silent nod of thanks. He stared long upon her path, even after she had vanished amid deep shadow. Chuck finally shook his thoughts back to the task at hand. The blade flashed faster than ever, amid new ambitions that felt so familiar, of building a better homestead for her.

Dinner was quiet, save for his apology, "I'm sorry if I made you feel awkward today. I won't do that again."

His offer was met with an appreciative turning of dimples he'd not noticed before, and he found himself grinning as well. Still, she offered little conversation, so much was she taken in thoughts, he knew she wouldn't share. When Chuck offered to dry the dishes, she waved him away explaining that he would need his sleep, if he was going to keep working like that. He could have pointed out her working as hard, but obediently retreated to his tent.

He did feel tired, and the fading light soothed him, but the night was hot, and muggy. The perspiration would not leave him, so that finally, he rose to go to the river. The thick chestnut leaned out over mild currents, which bent round the cabin, standing so close to wet sand. There were also bushes reaching right to the shore, with ample limbs for hanging clothing. This he did, before easing himself into shallows, which felt rather warm. Wading out chest deep, he let himself plunge under, then kick back to where a hand stretched below could touch the river bed. There anchored by his fingertips, he let his body float, smiling at the gentle pull of the current upon him.

His eyes shot open at a disturbance in the water, just beyond the bend. Moonlight lit the surface like a silver crescent, so that all was easy to see. She had done the same, and was to her neck, before he saw her, as she made for deeper water in slow, gentle strokes. It was then she stopped, seeming to sense him.

Turning slowly, Helen sighted the man. Her expression did not change, nor did she speak a word, but made her way toward him. He knew she was gaining the shallows, but she kept the water at her neck. Then Helen stopped, and silence held the night. Her eyes were riveted on his, and for a moment she seemed to falter, but suddenly stood in a spray of froth. He felt a shock run through his own body, as he noted rivulets tracing paths all round her breasts, and down each slight curve of her abdomen. Still, she rose from the water, coming on in a determined stride, as she reached behind her head to loosen the silver clasp, which had held her hair up all day. Those soft golden strands cascaded down her back, and around one slender shoulder, to barely cover a glistening nipple.

Without a word, he rose from the waters, to draw Helen into his arms. Their lips lingered close for a moment, and then they gave in to that first kiss, which set his mind to swirling.

His lids were red in sunlight, as he felt a blanket plop upon him. Chuck stirred to shield his eyes, but a man's voice sounded loud nearby, "Rest easy son. Rest easy."

Blinking against the light, he saw Edgar leaning close over him. A feeble attempt to sit up proved beyond the lad, as all he could mumble was, "Wha- what?"

"I said rest easy,' Edgar groused, 'I reckon you got bloody pneumonia, layin' about in your underwear like that. Damned idiot!"

In spite of the hot sun, Chuck was freezing, and

covered in sweat, so that he figured the old man was right. Further admonishment had him cringing, "You'd better have strength to get in the truck, then it's straight to the hospital! I'll bring the truck right here. Hope that grave don't collapse."

As the old man walked away, Chuck tried to focus on his surroundings, and sure enough, he was flat on his back, beside the pit, where Helen lay. He made a point of not looking in, preferring to savor those visions still gracing his fevered mind. As the man seemed to take forever with his truck, Chuck found himself longing for one ladle full of water, and when Edgar finally arrived, he found the lad weakly mumbling, "Don't waste it! Don't waste it."

Shaking his hoary head, he did his best to help Chuck into the passenger seat. There was no bother with the seat belt, but great care taken in that old blanket totally enclosing his patient. The door sounded like a gong, and Edgar came round in what for him was a terrible hurry. The engine roared, and they set off. In his greatest urgency, the old man didn't drive anything like John, but it still seemed fast on a bumpy road. There was silence for a time, but it didn't last, as the driver announced, "I used to think I saw her ghost, you know. My great grandma. Saw her a few times, walking the shoreline; lookin' at the water. Used to think she was lookin' for her gravestones."

The old man cast an urgent scrutiny of the barely conscious youth shivering near him, before continuing in an easier tone, "Story came down, of a stranger who passed through here. Had her with child, then just vanished. The birth was hard, and she was all alone. Only the old Chief coming by saved her, but she didn't live many years after. Used ta' hate red heads for that."

Chuck couldn't be bothered to turn his head, but kept quiet through a mild shock, which swept his body again. He

welcomed the silence, to follow, content to peer into the
mirror outside his door, for it offered occasional glimpses of
that place he'd come to know. He held fast to the valley as
long as he could, even though a mist formed across his eyes.
Yet it was all his, blue water held in an emerald embrace,
and the lady standing at it's shore, until the high crest took
it.

ON A PRESSING PROBLEM

By the High Office of Melkhanna
High Wizard of the North Wind
Curator of Archives
Region of Bolchor proper

Release to His Highness
Rogalton
King of Krunalsys

Your Majesty

It is my great honor, to receive your latest correspondence, regarding affairs in this region. I trust that my report will lighten your heart, and ease your worry. I felt compelled, however, to use this separate parchment, in the treatment of a rather thorny issue.

In truth, we have had attacks, losing the better part of a village, only last week. The immediate response is a simple one, to exterminate if possible, (a scenario, which relies on individual courage, above all else) and yet, is that the best solution? Before we leap to a set course, we must gather all scholars knowledgeable in such things, to truly ponder, and debate the great questions.

What is a Dragon?

What is its relation to the world?

Is ours the only world that matters, or can they exist apart from us?

When all is said, and done, what damage do dragons really do, in relation to their own presence to us, and longevity?

Must we exterminate? (Can we exterminate?) And if so,

how many are still left, after the exuberant efforts of our forefathers?

Where can they be found?

If successfully exterminated, what would our world be like, without dragons?

And lastly,

can they, instead, be controlled?

I can guess, the last question piques your Majesty's curiosity most readily. And yet, with apologies, I must take these matters in order, lest my essay fall to ridicule among my scholarly peers.

What is a Dragon?

This may seem a simple question, but seeing as those who've survived encounters with the creatures, are almost as rare as dragons themselves, could we not be too hasty in our assessment?

Yes, they are vast, winged brutes, who fly down out of our mountains, faster than the winds from the north, to burn practically everything they look at, once they've snatched enough livestock. Those feeding young, are by far the worst, as their visits are multiple, so that nothing is usually left standing. I was on hand, at a recent attack, where upon gazing up at those distant shining scales, and massive wings spread wide, I ardently hoped it was just a cranky old bachelor! Still, I could find a place in my heart, to ponder the possible fate of the creatures, which brings me to the next question.

What is it's relation to the world?

Sadly, most of our species cannot think of any kind of relation with a dragon. Yet, the question more to the point is what is their relation to the world; not us. It was said long ago, that our ancients used to go on pilgrimage to vast caves, and there, consult the great wisdom offered by those timeless creatures. In moments of great distress, when all other avenues were exhausted, even Kings themselves, would make the trek, for wondrous, and often impeccable guidance. Something happened, however, all but forgotten in our times, but terrible enough to rend that ancient, and cherished bond between dragons, and our ancestors.

Now, it seems, we have no use for them, and they in turn have apparently forgotten any good feeling derived from offering anything useful to our kind. So, the question more to the point is this; have we both lost our way? Are Dragon's so removed from their grand, and wondrous for bearers, that they have no lasting sensation of self worth? Does this prompt the attacks, and if so, is there any way to remind them of their great heritage, in hopes of a halt to this destruction?

In the meantime, other than their introducing charcoal to our environs, thus replenishing the soil, (and it could well be pointed out, we do get very good harvests, for some years after a Dragon attack) most people see no benefit in having a Dragon around.

Still, in addressing the next point, who is the more selfish being. If I may be so bold, as your Majesty knows well that I do not direct this at your person, but at our kind in general, it really begs the question; is our world the only one that matters? Can we not see our way clear to a world shared with them? If the changing of the Dragon mind set is possible, can they not exist in unison with our everyday efforts, or even apart, as some wondrous, and distant being adorning our skies, from time to time? Even if this is not achieved, we really must face an oft ignored question:

"What damage does a Dragon REALLY do, in relation to it's own presence to us, and average longevity?"

If you consider the vast life span of a Dragon, (and indeed the 'younger' ones have had dealings with your own ancestry, from time to time) the actual damage done by each individual is surprisingly minimal! In fact, I risk seeming rather controversial, in pointing out my having known some men of conquest, who have donned armor to wreak far more destruction in this world, in far less time than any Dragon to my knowledge. Indeed, in my two hundred plus cycles of the seasons, I've known those who've died as little more than boys, having razed entire cities, and plundered realms. As your Majesty is a great man of conquest, I hasten to add that yours, is a truly noble cause of expanded learning, and I'll elaborate no further on this point.

Shall we get straight to the thorny issue of extermination? Must we exterminate, and if this decision is reached, CAN we exterminate?

If we consider the amount of attacks per Dragon, per thousand year period of its' life, the result could be counted on one hand. This is known by a system of calculation started by Norelea, the High Sorceress, some seven centuries past. She compiled ancient accounts of Dragon sightings, and some ballads left over from times before the rift between our species. Coupling these with accounts current to her own time, and her own sightings, she could positively identify two of the creatures, by some physical peculiarity, or other, now forgotten. Both are now gone from us, the one being confirmed dead some three centuries past, while the other simply vanished, never to be seen since the time of Norelea herself.

At present, we have four identified Dragons, none of which are responsible for the current spate of attacks. That 'honor' belongs to an unknown visitor, who did turn out to be a loner. We've yet to discover its' area of dwelling, but though this is not a task for the faint hearted, I assure your Majesty, that we will. When we do, however, should we seek to slay the beast, or even enter into a long, and concerted effort to treat each creature in kind? MUST we exterminate? My people may well be accused of being nestled in ivory towers, but ours is an active system, of far reaching investigation, and our endeavors suggest tolerance.

At this point I hope your Majesty will tolerate a rather sizable aside, but I should point out that our towers are mostly marble, though there is one made of a boney substance we cannot yet identify. There are those who say it is made of the bones of one, or more ancient Dragons, which used the aerie as their home. In

truth, it does have some rather thorny protrusions, while its'
arched dome appears to be of fused Dragon scales. These are so
faded by age, as to be rather milky in appearance, even at night,
and nearly transparent. In truth, it is a most pleasant place to be,
as the dome let's through such a soft, amber radiance by day, and
seems to enhance moonlight, so that one can read at any hour.
Though much more harsh, and rather eerie in appearance, as
compared to the generally smooth features of our fortress, it is,
none the less, among the more calming elements of our home.

Until, however, I can retrieve an actual Dragon bone, it's
construction must be held in speculation only. In the meantime, the
many wanderers we receive, who stray so far off the beaten path,
to witness the wonders of Bolchor, seem to remember that tower
best. Therefore, I am little surprised that talk of ivory towers has
spread far, and wide. I hear that there are even sketches, and
paintings of our home adorning tavern walls, as far away as
Krolnaar! I am not certain we should be flattered. There are those,
who speak of shutting the fortress from outsiders, to stem this
misrepresentation, and also to end the unwanted attention of those
who seek ivory, much to their peril in this place. I myself, believe it
will only add to the misunderstanding, while the thieves who try
knocking pieces off of our tower, are normally caught, and
disintegrated on the spot. I myself have had to dispatch three of
the rogues in this manner. It is rather draining, and a bit too
dramatic for my tastes. I do prefer feeling much more chipper, as I
enter the library to tackle more scrolls. Couple that with the
aggravation of seeing yet another chunk struck off, and yes, I am
also tempted to shut the entire thing up. Still, despite growing
pressure, it is the belief of both myself, and our leader
Mylbacrooms, that what seem to be pilgrimages, should be allowed
to continue.

In regards now, to the beast, which attacked that village. It
is no doubt sated, and so we shall see no more of it for quite some
time, and probably not in my lifetime. I also surmise a general
rarity of visitation, in relation to their population. This is based on
my theory, that Dragons only come to us for easier kills, such as

penned livestock, when nesting, or severely ill. I point to our new acquaintance being extremely old, and prone to accept the easier flight offered by our lowlands. We are an item of convenience, to a feeble creature. This is not a wonderful prospect, but a reality in nature. Yet, this beast seemed stronger in its' last pass through these parts, and so, I think it will revert to hunting wild game.

Also, seeing as a Dragon's digestive system seems by all accounts, to be a ponderous thing, I venture to say this one won't be seen out of its' lair for an extremely long time.

A further point to be made, is our own use of magic. Any gathering of three, or more of my peers has produced combined skills capable of not only keeping a dragon at bay, but even causing the creature to leave off its' assault. I reluctantly must add two points. The latter result was only produced once, and it was myself leading the circle. I must also add, that the effort laid us all out, for who knows how many days. None of us were inclined to ask the locals how long we slept. You see, the mind of a Dragon is a vastly powerful thing, and not at all simple to sway.

Secondly, these effects are fleeting, and so, we are of limited use. Sometimes, the creature will fly away, as villagers cheer, only to come right back again, as we grace the high places surrounding their homes, trying what we can, but looking to all the world as idle slackers, while the dwellings burn. In light of these failures, it may seem easier to see the death of the things, and an end to the threat, but again, we are inclined to refuse this action. Yet, if it is your Majesty's wish, and there is little doubt you have no shortage of heroes, the task of killing Dragons must begin with one question.

CAN we exterminate them?

As the research of my order can put us in close proximity to a rather robust subject, I should add that in the humble opinion of this author, 'close proximity' begins, when one can make out the wing beats coming down a valley. Having made the acquaintance of parties of self proclaimed 'Dragon Slayers', soon to be found dead, I believe I can give a fair assessment that any such task is well nigh impossible.

That is, on the surface, at least; while in truth, even the most difficult of tasks is always 'possible', especially when survival is involved. It has also been my experience, that people are twice as grand as they think they are, while the most trying times only serve to help them meet that 'other person'. This observation will find its place later in my treatment. For now, I shall cling to the subject.

There is muttering of extermination, but in truth, the destruction of even a single Dragon is no mean feat. Consider the many weapons in their possession. The most critical of these, is the breath, and I mean that literally! Anyone who has hidden from view, while a giant muzzle pumped gushes of warm air, on just the other side of a boulder, could tell you that such breath alone could kill! I had no idea if I would vomit, and be incinerated, or simply lose consciousness, but somehow, my guts held, and I escaped detection.

As for that legendary flame, I have seen both horse, and rider appear from the dying of a glowing cloud, staying perfectly still, until the weight of their blackened, and twisted armor caused them to crumble into piles of ash. There wasn't a sound. It was like watching a statue fall apart.

Of course, only particularly peaked Dragons do that. Others like to do less cooking, and take their meals still screaming. Still others don't bother with fire at all, but spit a saliva, not so pleasant to deal with. Blistering, and blindness usually result, with the disoriented victim being pulverized by massive jaws, and fangs of a foot long, or better. (At this point, I should add that a Dragon's tooth makes a wonderful war horn, and even drinking horn, but these are so rare, as to be worth - if you'll pardon, a King's ransom.)

Now, come the claws. So swift are these, any unfortunate soul has little time to move, and usually can only place hope in an excellent shield, and armor. Still, a swat from a Dragon, can send a warrior sprawling, and open to further attack, with little time in the face of such ferocity, to re-establish a defense. If armor does fail, then the slicing tends to be equal to the crushing effect of so much power. Broken bones, and profuse bleeding are common.

The wings can do some harm as well, although these are only used in a most desperate pinch, for the use of these are kept to a minimum, by still another final weapon. Last, but not least, there comes the tail. Need I state the number of times I've seen the use of this? It is long enough, to seemingly strike out of nowhere, assuming the victim is still standing, after sampling aforementioned delicacies. Knowledge of the average damage these do, is sadly lacking, as the unfortunate individual is usually gobbled up, before being able to yell anything useful like, "Ooh, my broken ribs!"

Thus, the ongoing frustration of many an historian, but it is certain that anything struck by this protuberance goes flying like a leaf on the wind. It matters not, whether this be horse, man, or war dog. (I'll not mention women here. There are memories too close, and unsettling. The heart is still raw from it.) There are also some very old accounts, of the narrower part of the tail actually rending the smaller of those forms in twain. These accounts even go so far, as to suggest two particularly sadistic beasts specializing in achieving this supposedly desired result. One report even had a creature purring like a kitten, as it licked the gore off of its' tail! (I tell you, research is NOT for the faint of heart!) Generally, the tail is used to stun things considered edible by the Dragon. (And most things are.) It then scoops them toward that horrid maw, for a quick chomp, and swallow.

In short, I would not recommend Dragon Hunting as a hobby. Our research is dangerous enough, although it is as if some of their numbers have discerned our purpose as passive, and so, our casualties are mercifully few. This is advantageous, since we do not have the acolytes to lose. By sharp contrast, your Majesty certainly has the manpower, but I hasten to point out the cost of such a struggle. This endeavor could severely weaken your forces, thus inviting vain hopes of invasion by nearby kingdoms. I know from your reputation as a cunning strategist, that this is no doubt already debated.

I also can guess, you've thought of drawing each beast into open flight, and then showering it with projectiles. This brings us to yet another point about Dragons; their scales. It is true, that the yearlings have their plating, about equal to the thickness of tree bark. As such, it is as soft, as it will ever be in the creature's life. For this reason, you may well be able to bring down the young ones, but with a Dragon of maturity, the scales can be as thick as your hand. In that case, arrows, and even javelins will not penetrate, especially at distance. Also, since the beasts can close the length of the average javelin toss in a heartbeat, it is impossible to keep those valued troops out of the bite of a Dragon. Providing a shield wall for them to retreat through will result in terrible loss of life, even if the formation stands fast against such a massive, charging serpent. It is also a mistake to keep warhorses in close proximity to such a struggle, because even the most stalwart of those noble animals, have been known to lose composure at critical times. That is definitely not an acceptable distraction.

Further, to predict expected losses, from seeking to deal with everything a Dragon offers - time, and time again, it is of value to know how many there are. We calculate twenty, between your southern plains, and the Ice Needle Wastes, with their favored point of congregation being the mountains just north of this fortress. We have traced them westward, to the Great Spine, where it intersects our range, and though we have followed apparent migrations both north, and south for nearly it's entire length, we have seen no instance of their crossing over into the next kingdom. Of course if they do, we will NOT follow, for obvious reasons. And yet, they apparently prefer their ancient routes, and haunts in your lands. Perhaps they feel safest here.

It is ironic that this fortress is so venerable, as to possess a very impressive aviary, dating back to those long forgotten days, when our two species enjoyed that aforementioned bond. The high platform has long since been turned into a peaceful garden, perfect for watching the suns run our valley's length, setting the river molten, as they pass their watch over to the night. In fact there are still shards of egg shell, some as large as a shield, to be found among the foliage, adorning that quiet place. The very name of our fortress, "Bolchor" is said to be that of the last great Dragon to sire its' young on these heights. In those days, Kings from many lands came to this silent, watchful rock, to seek the guidance of Bolchor. Unfortunately, this location is so remote, we haven't had a King here since, but our lands are exceedingly beautiful, and mostly serene. If I may be so bold, as to suggest, your Majesty really should visit; at his convenience, of course. I believe my King would enjoy the wild, and quiet splendor of this place.

Please excuse my rambling, for I know my peers would not. Now to the topic at hand - where to find them. It is not enough to simply point to the mountains, when a few have even been stumbled upon, curled up, and fast asleep amid the lush foliage of small valleys. Needless to say, any foolish enough to startle these beasts to wakefulness, have been responsible for the most intriguing patterns of twisted, leaning tree trunks, trampled grasses, and brush, and churned up chunks of soil. Couple that with the usual splash of crimson on the green, in contrast to smouldering black splotches scattered about, and the result can be rather artistic. I doubt, however, that the sources of inspiration much enjoyed such a creation.

Turning once again to the mountains, they are found in any number of caves, and crags. Some have dwellings high in the peaks, while others hold their retreat in the bowels of the world. Most of these places are deep, and sometimes akin to a maze. Numbers of these can be vigorously searched to disappointing effect, even though the Dragon is not far off. Some of these give the uncomfortable impression of having been deliberately chosen to turn the hunter into the hunted. Hence, the boulder aforementioned.

It is said Dragons can smell gold, and don't at all mind rootling around the deepest places, for the longest time, as they use their claws to gouge out veins of every size. How they can carry it back to their lair is anyone's guess, but it is the theory of this author, that they pack it in their mouths, much like a chipmunk. As most Dragons in my observation are quite without

*pockets, I consider this a rather sound estimation. There have
however, been a few shards found, about the size, and shape of my
forefinger, which I reckon to have come free from claws, en route
to various lairs. These finds are rare, since Dragons are quite
thorough in cleaning up after themselves. Still, I can boast
possession of a few of these fragments, which do have great effect
upon the parchment, when winds howl up the valley, and through
these tower windows.*

    *Once brought to the lair, these gold scrapings are spread
out like a massive mattress. You can imagine this requires frequent
trips, which partly explains why Dragons are rarely seen. This is
also because they seem to lounge upon their creations forever,
getting no end of enjoyment out of the beds they build.*

    *Of course, I tell your Majesty nothing new, as this is the
stuff of children's stories. Therefore, my sharing of such
'revelations' do not endanger them any more than usual. Indeed,
Dragon hoards have been the driving force behind countless
expeditions, spanning forgotten millennia. Thus, my theory that
this is a probable cause for the great rift between us now. In fact,
there are whisperings across the mists of time, held, and hinted at
in nearly forgotten ballads, of a first breach of trust, and murder.
The poor victim was a Dragon doomed by it's trust. From that,
open animosity has turned the ensuing struggle into something of a
noble pursuit, forging heroes of great fame through the centuries
since.*

    *This has resulted in a rather solitary race, which like to set
dwellings in the deepest, darkest, and furthest reaches of their
respective haunts. They do tend to gravitate to these places, when
they know they are dying. Also, their young do not disturb their
remains, but wall up their ancestry, bed, and all. For this reason, I
can well imagine many magnificent skeletons, preserved in
darkness.*

    *To close this phase of instruction, your Majesty can easily
see the frustrating prospects ahead, should this rumored course by
taken. Whether successful, or not, any trek into a Dragon's lair,
even a very understanding one, can test the stoutest heart. I do*

acknowledge, however, that my Sire has the brave souls to attempt this, but must add that the high places are no less perilous. Far more common is it, where rock, and ice are one, to have men fall uselessly to their doom, having never even seen a Dragon. Yet, is the sighting any better, when such a beast appears to use all of its' 'gifts', or simply hurl people to their deaths?

Still, we must entertain the next logical step in our progression. I know the might of your men. I have visited court enough to gauge the security of this kingdom. Indeed, as I write this, I know another enemy realm falls, the only question being, did its' sovereign survive? I know well the sound of battle, and can yet hear the urgency in the voices of so many doomed on the field. Drumbeats sound in the distance, but cannot shield their piteous calls. It is as if they not only say farewell, but greet something we cannot see, waiting just for them, in some other world. These things never change. Again, we are victorious.

There is something strange about complete success. I dare say, something unnatural. Yet if, and when we manage to kill every last creature, what is there left to fear? What then? What would our world be like without Dragons? We will certainly have no burnings, nor will we have massacres. There will be no wary eye turning toward distant peaks. Indeed, we shall live in a world where battle horns sound no longer, lest our own kind more frequently bring strife against us. Whatever shall we do? What a boring place to be!

The crops will fail. That is for certain. People will lose their respect for the world around them, and begin to think they can conquer it! Can you believe such madness could sweep the realms? There is something sinister to me, that we might eventually consider ourselves as the masters of all we survey, with absolutely nothing to oppose us. If such a time is to come, will we be better than the Dragons? Is it possible, that we are ready to cast aside, the truest, and best custodians of our world?

Really, no matter who it is; whether or not clan, and kin were lost to the beasts, who has not marveled at the bellow of a Dragon? Who has not been bedazzled, by the glint of so many scales, catching sun, or moonlight? Who has not felt diminished, as those great wings stretch wide, to gather massive gusts of wind, and drive such a slender form ever forth? Who has not been shaken to the marrow, and yet somehow resisted feeling privileged? I have looked into the eyes of a Dragon, only to be frozen by a wisdom I cannot fathom! To live without all of that - whatever shall we do?

I cannot help, but feel, we could lose something great; a power we can never know again. I'll not think on it any longer.

Can they be controlled? (Ah, yes - the question.) The answer is 'yes'! That is, of course, if certain events transpire. (To be dealt with shortly.) If Dragons were simply controlled, it would be a sad enterprise. For something so noble, and powerful to behave as an automaton would be tragic. Yet, there is something. In this, we must trust to legend, in winning through to a world, where Dragons hold fast their magnificence, and yet benefit us by their own choosing. It can be, as it once was, with the rift forgotten! (Well, at least ignored.)

Here, I make mention of the slimmest of margins, on which all hope resides. There is an item, or rather a man who holds such. This man is, or rather was the last of a most ancient order, which stayed allied to the beasts, when the great rift occurred. For some long forgotten reason, the Dragons did not reject those folk. Old tales hint at the founder of their caste, trying to stop the murder, and looting, which led to the split.

At any rate, this order was said to possess golden torques of radiance, gifted to them, by the beasts themselves. Furthermore, these torques are said to have a certain connection with, and influence over all of their kind. The extent of this influence is unknown, but it could be something as simple as recognition of the bearer of such an item, as an ally unquestioned. These Torques are instantly recognizable, being ornately carved of red gold, to glow like flame, even in dim light.

Also, any bearer of such a thing, can understand the language of Dragons, carved by claws throughout time in the very rock. Riddles, parables, ballads, poems; all made clear to any who wear that fabled gold! Imagine the knowledge gained in such a way! Truly Sire, we may well be on the verge of something great!

"How do we find such wondrous things," you may ask. Let me take you back, my king, to that single, aforementioned personage. As a child, I heard of a man of great age, even then, who rode Dragons! My little head held the vision of that long grey beard catching the gusts, and streaming behind him, as man, and beast passed before a full moon. At times like that, it was said his laughter would echo down long valleys, but otherwise, he was a most dour character. There was even talk of folk seeking him out, never to be seen again. It was whispered, that he would visit death upon those too curious, rather than suffer intrusion. He certainly was known to wield great magic, which he readily demonstrated whenever any drew too close to his Dragon friends, especially the very young.

Those who had seen him, and survived, namely women, children, and the elderly, mentioned soft, yet piercing blue eyes, made all the more startling, in contrast to a long black mane. These stories are obviously contemporary to his youth, and that all but predates our written history. By far, his most familiar incarnation, places him as a decidedly elderly presence, wandering the scarps, and fissures of the canyon lands north of our range. It is conveniently remote, as I do not believe that entire expanse to have known a modern footfall. It is a desolate area, to be shunned by any sane mind. Thus, I can think of no place better, in which to search.

Is he alive? Is there anyone to search for? It should be noted, that most of his lore, spans perhaps two thousand years, and he was considered extremely old, when I was yet a young sniveling, still mulling over my first spell. Yet, it is said he is connected to them in all things, including their longevity. Therefore, I hold out great hope, that he may yet live. I must again make mention, however, that his disposition was long considered to rival even the grumpiest of his reptilian brethren. Couple this with his legendary penchant for throwing masses of spells, at any unfortunates, he decided not to like, (which included pretty much everybody) and that makes for some rather uncomfortable prospects. He may well have us wondering why we ever 'wanted' to find him. There is, however, a whispering in me, which believes he senses a gathering of clouds over his kind, and the need for cooperation. As such, he may be receptive to my proposal.

His name, is forgotten to time. For lack of a name, my parents merely dubbed him the "Dragon Master", or "Master of Dragons" depending on who was telling the tale. Of course, they used him to great effect, in keeping my siblings, and myself in line. Needless to say, we survived the retribution doled out to all naughty children. (Which never explained why certain true 'darlings' of our town survived to adulthood. I do admit to being sorely tempted at times, to aid the Dragon Master in his good works. But, I digress.)

If it please your Majesty, I would like to organize an expedition of hearty souls, capable of exploring those vast wastes of the north. I admit, this could be a task to span years, if the party is not killed outright. I also acknowledge, that this could lead to certain death. I do seek to shift the odds by insuring the participation of our order in this quest. I would like to go myself, but I have seen a very long life, so that my own progress may well slow them down. My diminished condition could well be the doom of this enterprise. And yet, I feel I must bear the brunt of my own idea. After all, my learned host to the north, is likely in similar condition, by ratio, and ignoring Dragon years, and if he can do it, why not I? Besides, if he seeks to greet us with fire, and thunder, then I would like nothing better than to meet him spell for spell. This anticipated wizards duel would only last a few spells, in my estimation, before mutual respect is reached, and constructive conversation ensues. Thus, is the way of our kind.

Now, I must add, that I have selected (at least in my mind) a fairly strong party, made up of some locals. They really have no idea why I linger over my pipe smoke in watching them, but you can well believe these wilds produce some very resourceful characters of stalwart resolve. The supply of a prolonged journey is not a problem either, as they are naturally familiar with our extensive network of alpine trade. In fact, two of them have been involved in that pursuit themselves. Of course, I reserve openings for whatever of your Majesty's men, or women you choose to assign, should you see fit to grant this expedition.

In closing Sire, I believe it advantageous to visualize a world 'with' Dragons. Imagine the serenity of a village actually guarded by one. Imagine the swiftness with which you could attend the most pressing problems of your realm! Even the most far flung reaches of the kingdom could be reached within two days, with yourself seated on the shoulders of their most magnificent beast! Could you imagine a more potent deterrent against raids on your borders? Further, if pressed on multiple fronts, in such a manner, you could oversee multiple battles, even at great distances from one another. That is if there is an enemy still standing fast, after seeing something so grand, bearing down on the field. You may well land, to merely address the pursuit of a routing army.

This next point may sound trite, but it should be pointed out, that the heat generated by a Dragon, could have far reaching effects on our daily lives. One half hearted snort in the direction of an outstretched torch, could have a towns lamplighters making the rounds in no time. Bread could be ready much sooner to be sure, though we can expect some ruined loafs, until the technique is perfected. If there might be a swifter, and thus more merciful way to burn miscreants at the stake, I've yet to imagine it. Houses carrying plague could be very thoroughly dealt with, and no, I do not recommend this course while the people are still alive inside.

Now, consider a typically drafty castle. It is likely your Majesty is feeling the effects of such a chill messenger of pain, and discomfort, as you read this. I would put it to you, that any new fortress structure be made with a Dragon's lair at its' lowest level, with venting built into the inner walls. In this way, the warmth of a dozing Dragon can be felt in every room on cold nights. Conversely, on hot days, the vents need merely be shut.

Moreover, these fine animals must be allowed to come, and go as they please, with the understanding that the most trusted soldiery will stand watch at the entrance, to guard their mattresses, while they are gone. Moreover, the law for any would be robbers should be harsh, perhaps with any transgressors being tethered to columns within the lair itself. There, they will await the judgement of the one they sought to rob. Do not forget the wisdom of Dragons, thus allowing for the notion of mercy shown. I'll wager any survivors will never even think of such foolishness again. And yes, we can rediscover the guidance of what were, and may yet be unrivaled councillors. Of course, in times to come, one need only go down to the bedrock, rather than trek a very many leagues.

Now, I must admit there are other types of Dragons, who have other attributes, but I really believe the most useful ones, are those closest at hand. I mean, those Snow Dragons of the far north, may be welcome on extremely hot days, but then there's the housing of the creatures, and we can't just toss our regular Dragon from its' lair at certain times of the year. Imagine the ramifications of that tact! Besides, I shudder at the vision of masses of curious children all stuck by the tongue to the sides of those things! Also, those brutes are far off in another Kingdom entirely, and not likely very receptive to the idea of leaving their nice cool climate. So no - it's best to leave off such folly, and stick with a more streamlined plan. We've yet to accomplish this first task, and must bend all thought, and effort to it. By your decree, of course.

I thank your Majesty for your time in this matter, looking forward to your response, (which would come swiftly, I might add, had we a Dragon handy) and so I leave my King, with this last vision to ponder. Imagine yourself in a world of true security, where you feel a sudden chill, and find yourself thinking, "What's keeping that blasted Dragon?!"

I remain, as always,

your faithful servant Sire,

Melkhanna

ISBN 1553952979